Magic Pickle

VS. THE EGG POACHER

BY SCOTT MORSE

A (graphix) Chapter Book

AN IMPRINT OF

SCHOLASTIC

NEW YORK TORONTO LONDON AUCKLAND SYDNEY MEXICO CITY NEW DELHI HONG KONG BUENOS AIRES

Library of Congress Cataloging-in-Publication Data

Morse, Scott.
Magic Pickle vs. the Egg Poacher : a Graphix illustrated chapter book /
by Scott Morse. -- 1st ed.
p. cm.
1. Graphic novels. I. Title. II. Title: Magic Pickle versus the Egg Poacher.

PN6727.M678M37 2008
741.5'973--dc22

2007035247

ISBN-13: 978-0-439-87997-2
ISBN-10: 0-439-87997-3

10 9 8 7 6 5 4 3 2 1   08 09 10

First edition, March 2008
Printed in the U.S.A. 23

Edited by Sheila Keenan
Creative Director: David Saylor
Book Design by Charles Kreloff

Prologue

(or everything you need to know before you read this book)

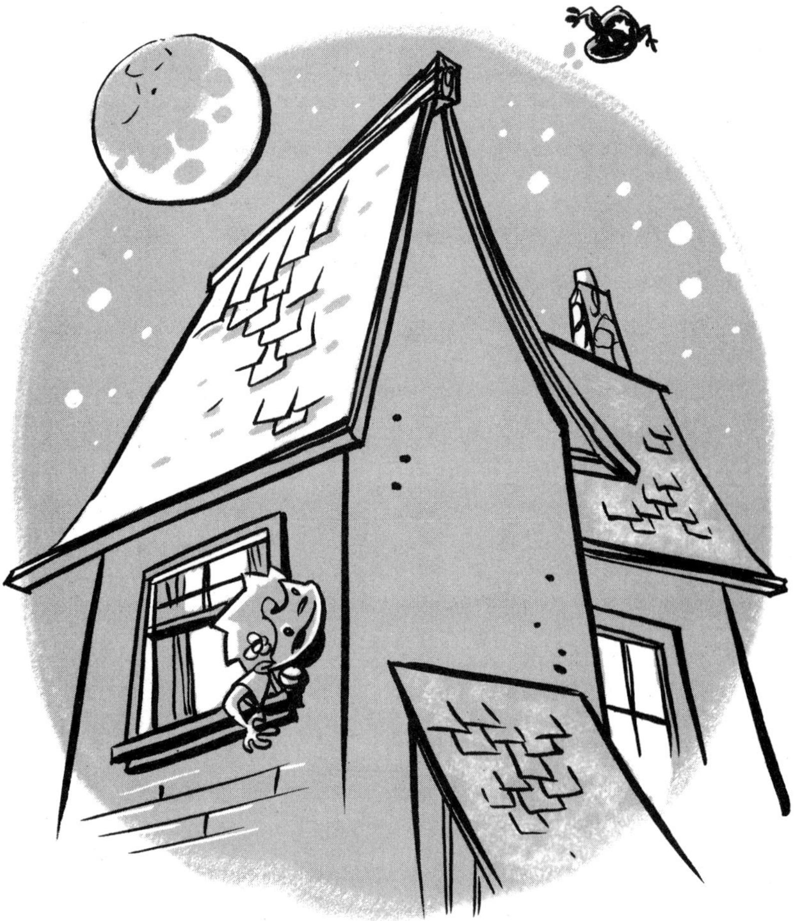

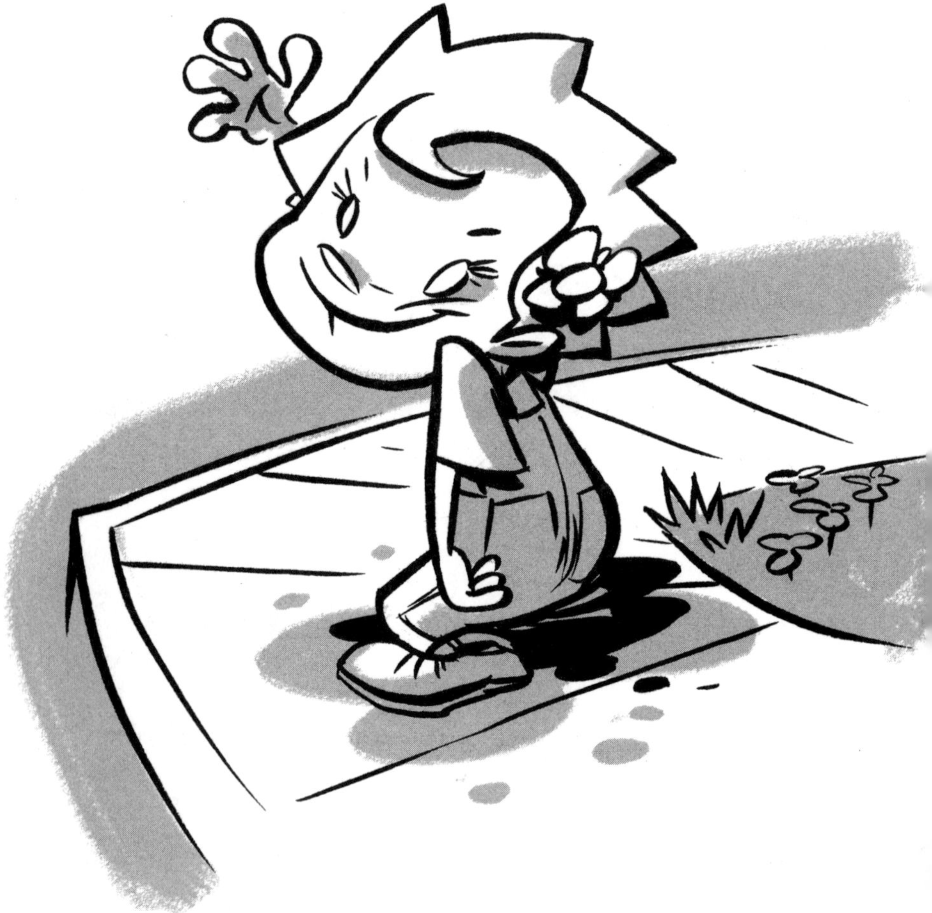

Jo Jo Wigman was like any girl you'd meet at school. Her dad was a top banana at Top Banana Computers and her mom was a top banana at home (who also happened to make one *mean* banana cream pie . . . but that's another story). Her brother, Jason, was just plain bananas. The Wigmans lived in a house much like every other house on their block, except for one thing:

There was a super-powered superhero living under Jo Jo's bedroom floor. Something stubby, green, and bumpy. Something that could fly. Something that looked just like . . .

A pickle!

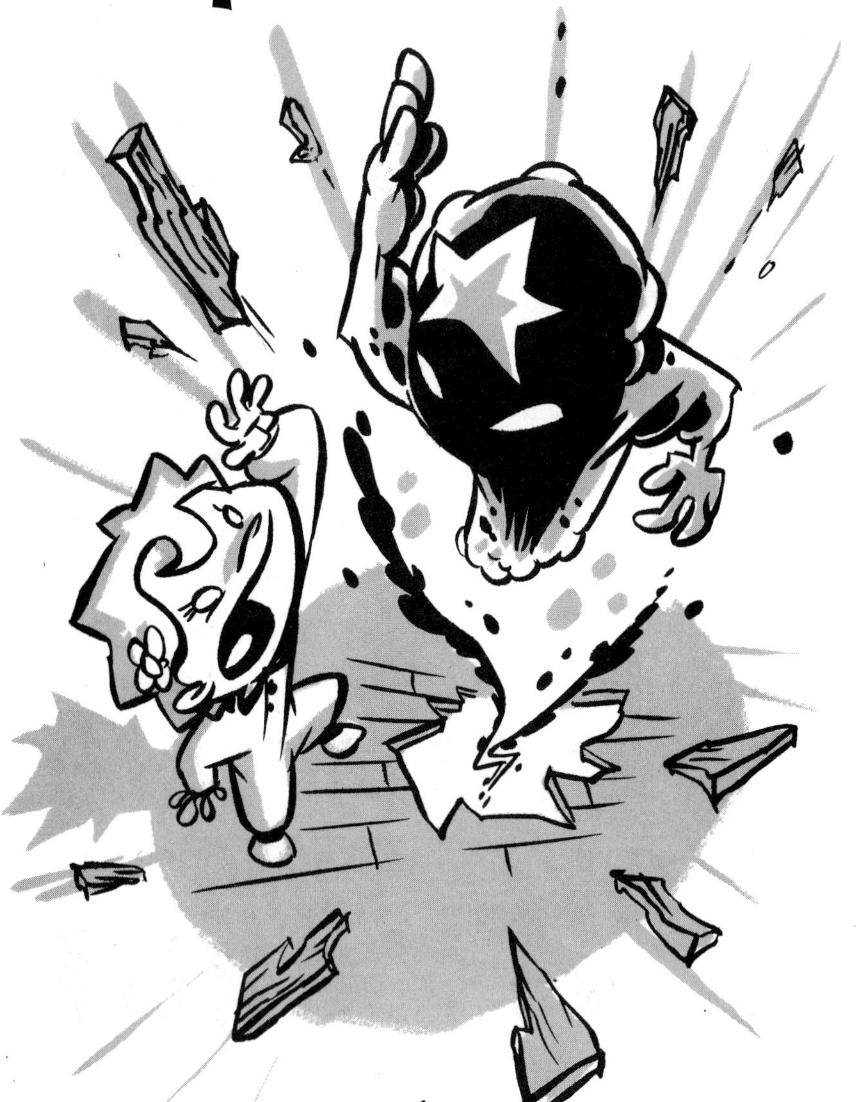

And this pickle could talk, too!

His code name was Weapon Kosher. He was an agent of dill justice. Jo Jo met him one night when he burst up through her bedroom floor. The briny superhero was in search of some vegetables gone bad: The Brotherhood of Evil Produce. All these super-charged fruits and veggies were created by a scientist named Dr. Jekyll Formaldehyde in a secret lab called Capital Dill. The lab was so secret that the government built a whole town on top of it. Jo Jo's room was right above the lab.

Down in Capital Dill, Dr. Formaldehyde was working on creating a special agent of justice, to fight crime and keep the world safe from rotten villains. One day, the pickle from his lunch accidentally fell into the experiment and . . .

KAZZZZORK!!!

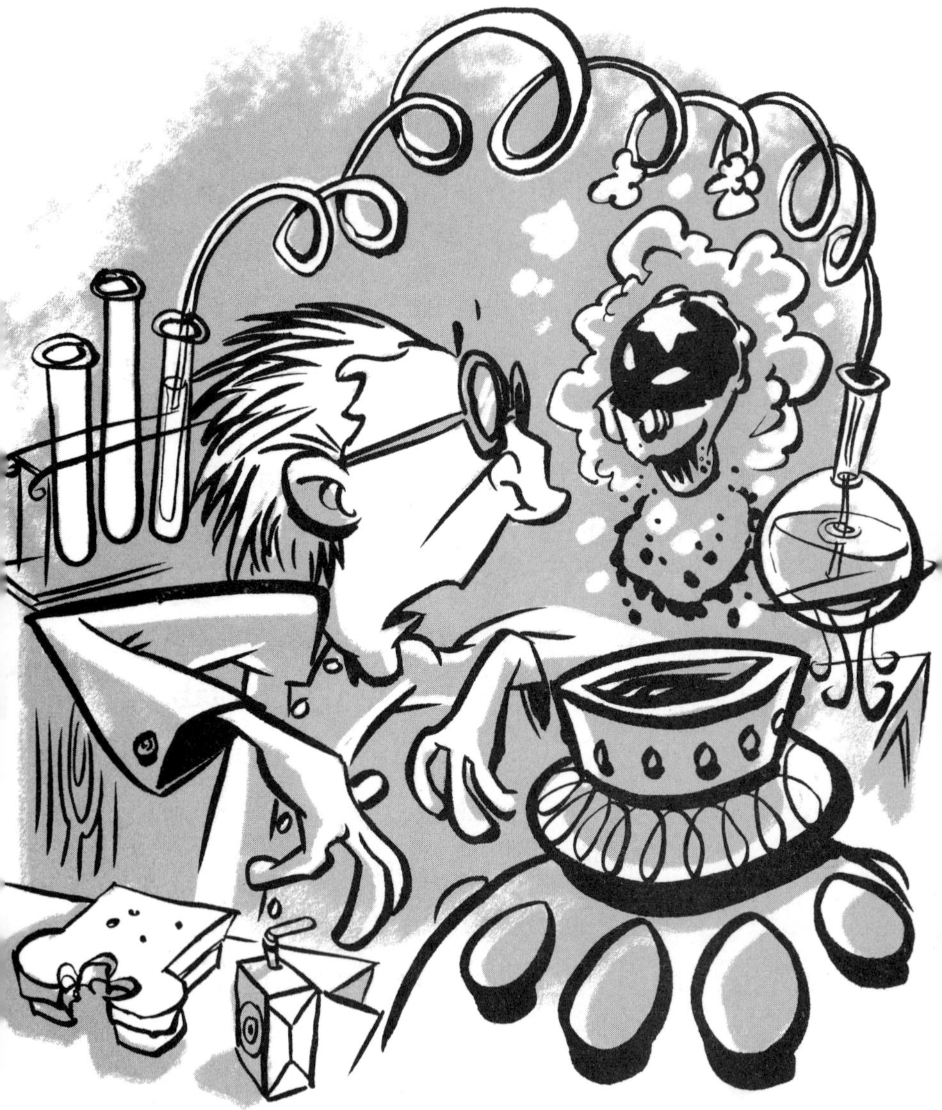

Weapon Kosher was born—but so was something else. . . .

BOOM!

The good doctor tried to transform his vegetarian combo lunch into an army of super-powered sidekicks for Weapon Kosher. Things went sour when radon rays from the gamma particle confibulator struck the veggies!

Dr. Formaldehyde's dream of creating a legion of super-powered heroes had become a *bad* dream—a nightmare! Dr. F. had accidentally created The Brotherhood of Evil Produce! The Brotherhood had only one goal: to take over the planet and bring forth the Salad Days, a new age in which fruits and veggies would rule the world, and people would have to find some other food group to balance their diets.

The Brotherhood of Evil Produce grew larger every minute! Rotten, rancid bad guys joined ranks: the Phantom Carrot, the Romaine Gladiator, Chili Chili Bang Bang, and more. Only Weapon Kosher could stop these grocery-cart convicts!

Dr. Formaldehyde launched himself into space in a special satellite. He circled the earth, tracking the no-good food group and sending news of their tasteless plans back to his kosher dill cohort in the secret

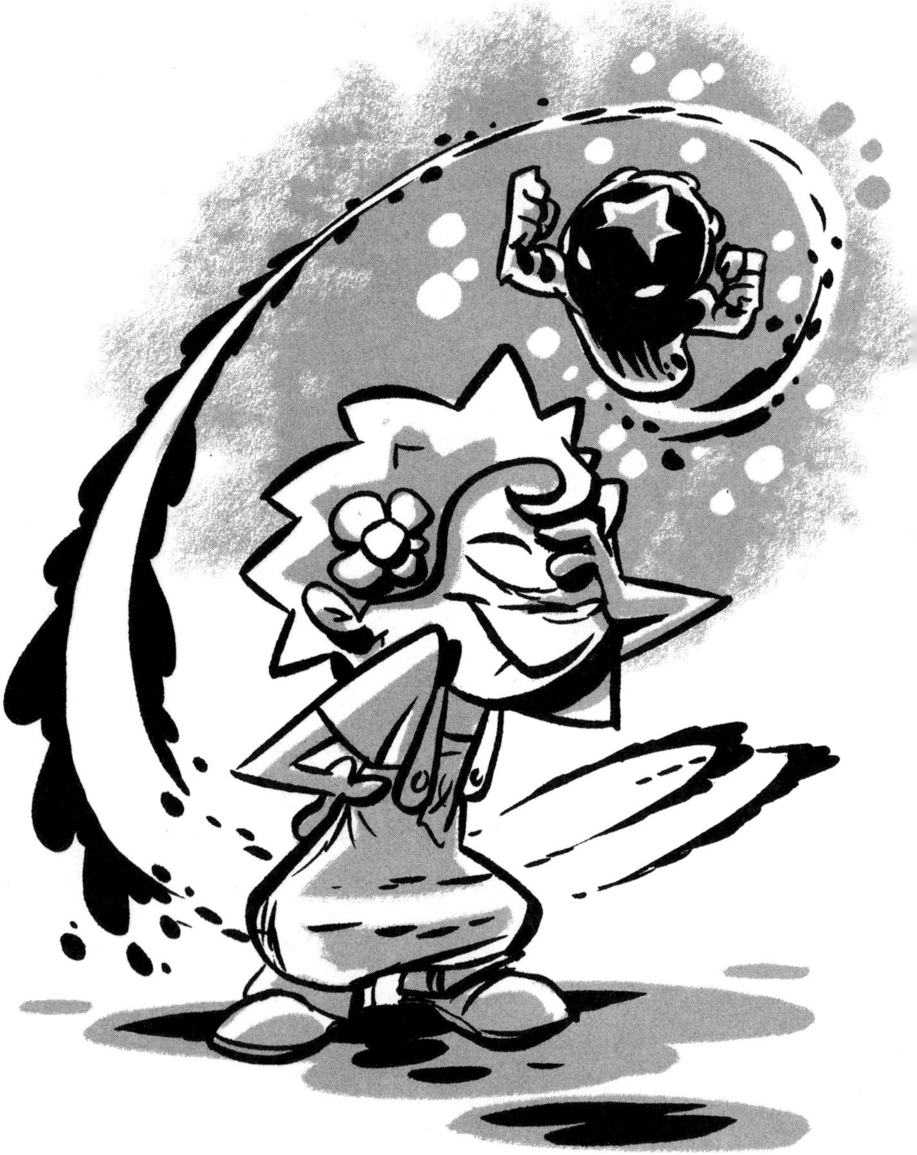

lab in Capital Dill. It was up to Dr. F.'s super-powered pickle to save the world—from under Jo Jo's bedroom floor!

And that's how Jo Jo came to share her room with the hush-hush, top-secret, relish-flinging, fast-flying Weapon Kosher superhero.

She liked to call him the Magic Pickle. It rolled off the tongue better.

Chapter 1

"Tomorrow is going to be so cool!" said Jo Jo. She skipped quickly alongside her best friend, Ellen Cranston. Their pal Mikey Spuchins trotted close behind. Each kid clutched a piece of paper.

"I've never been to the zoo before!" Ellen said. "I've never even *seen* a real-live wild animal, unless you count Mikey!"

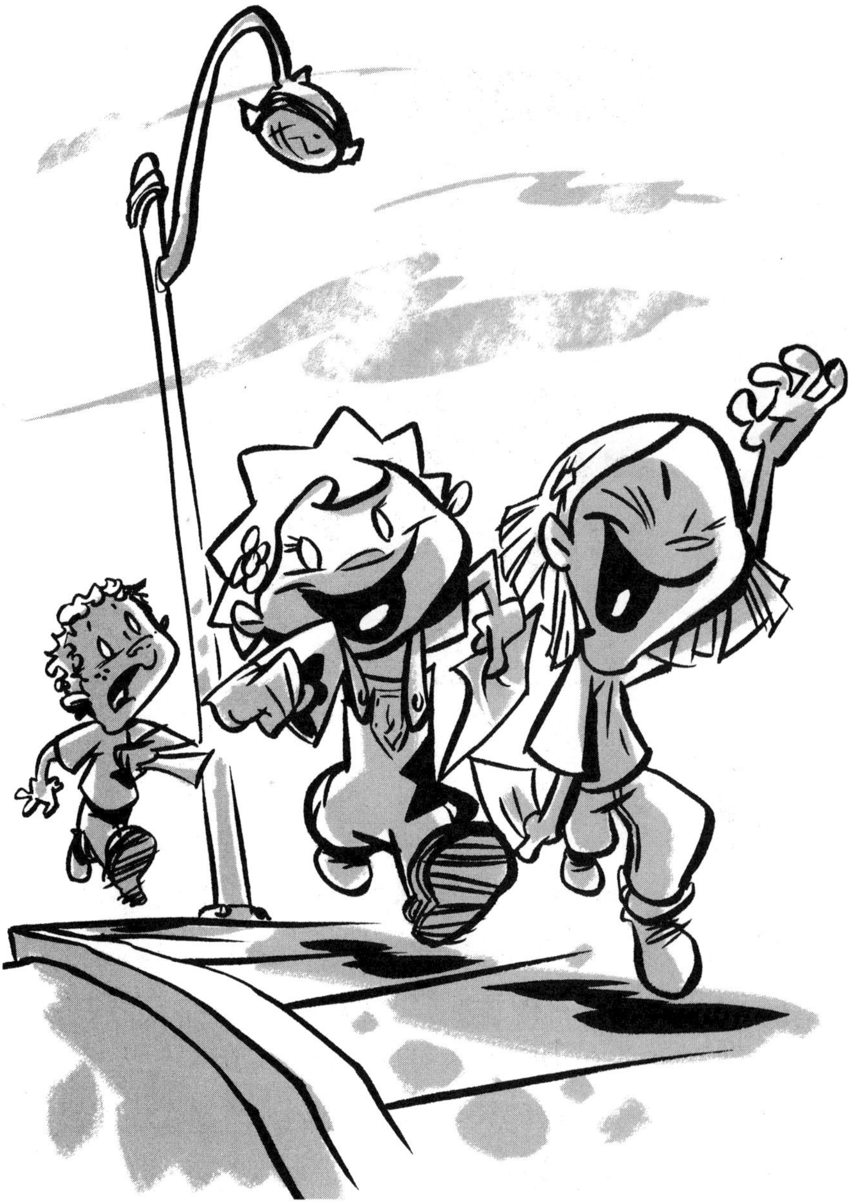

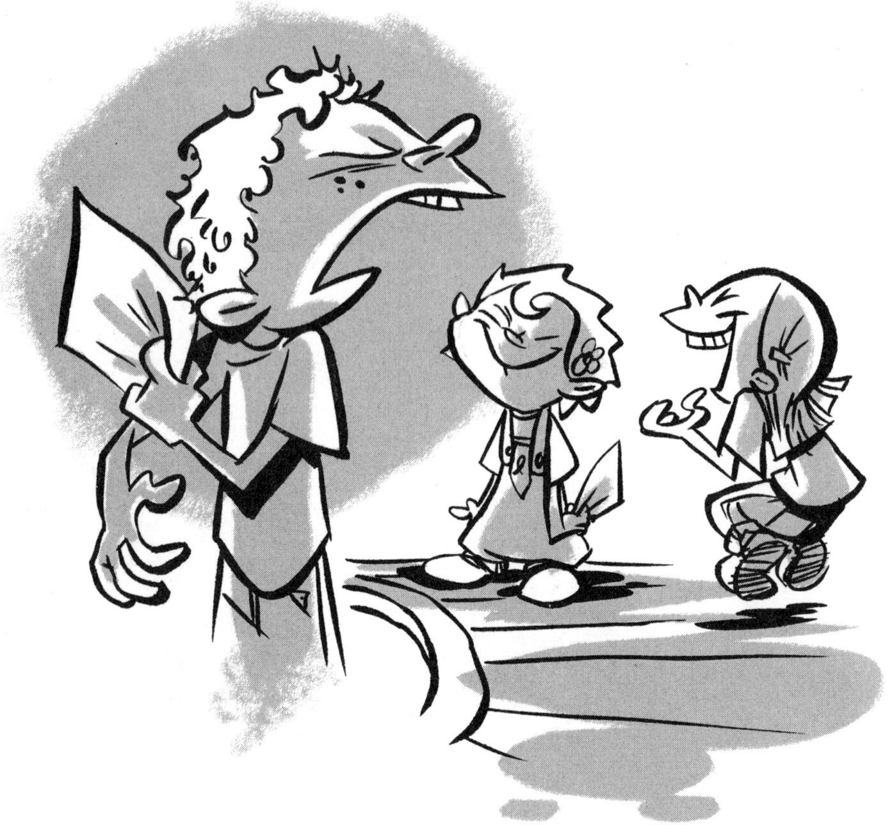

"Oh, HAW HAW, very funny!" mocked Mikey. "HAW HAW HAW."

"I guess he does kind of sound like a hyena," giggled Jo Jo as they quickened their pace.

"Or a *donkey*!" added Ellen.

"You guys are hilarious," Mikey groaned.

"I'll be sure to tell the monkeys at the zoo that I saw their hilarious cousins being hilarious."

"Just be sure to get your permission slip signed so we can all sit together on the bus," reminded Jo Jo. "We'll help you practice your hyena talk so you'll fit in with *your* long-lost family."

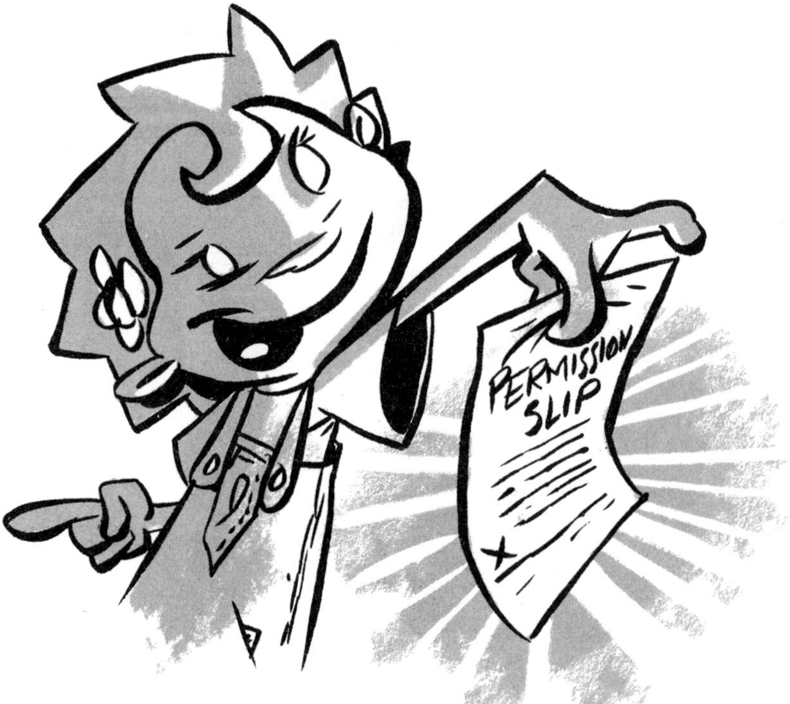
PERMISSION SLIP

"HAW HAW HAW," laughed Mikey.

When they reached their block, Jo Jo, Ellen, and Mikey split up and ran to their own homes.

Jo Jo burst into her house, excitedly slamming open the door.

"Mom! Come sign this thing!" she hollered.

"WHOA!" cried Mrs. Wigman when Jo Jo ran straight into her. "What's the ruckus all about?"

"Our class is going to the zoo tomorrow. You gotta sign this thing, you gotta sign it so I can get on the bus. Can you sign it, Mom? Can you? Sign it, please?!" Jo Jo sputtered. She could hardly catch her breath between words.

"Slow down, slow down!" laughed Mrs. Wigman. "I'll sign it on one condition."

"Anything! I'll do anything!" Jo Jo pleaded.

"Clean your room, spotless, before dinner," said her mother. "Then I'll see if I can find a pen with some ink in it to sign your slip."

Jo Jo raced up the stairs in a flash.

Chapter 2

Jo Jo flung open her bedroom door and stopped short. Clothes and toys lay in heaps all over the floor. Stacks of books had toppled over. Piles of stuffed animals completely blocked the closet door. Her bed was entirely covered with dirty laundry and wide-open comic books.

"This place is a pigsty!" Jo Jo winced. "I

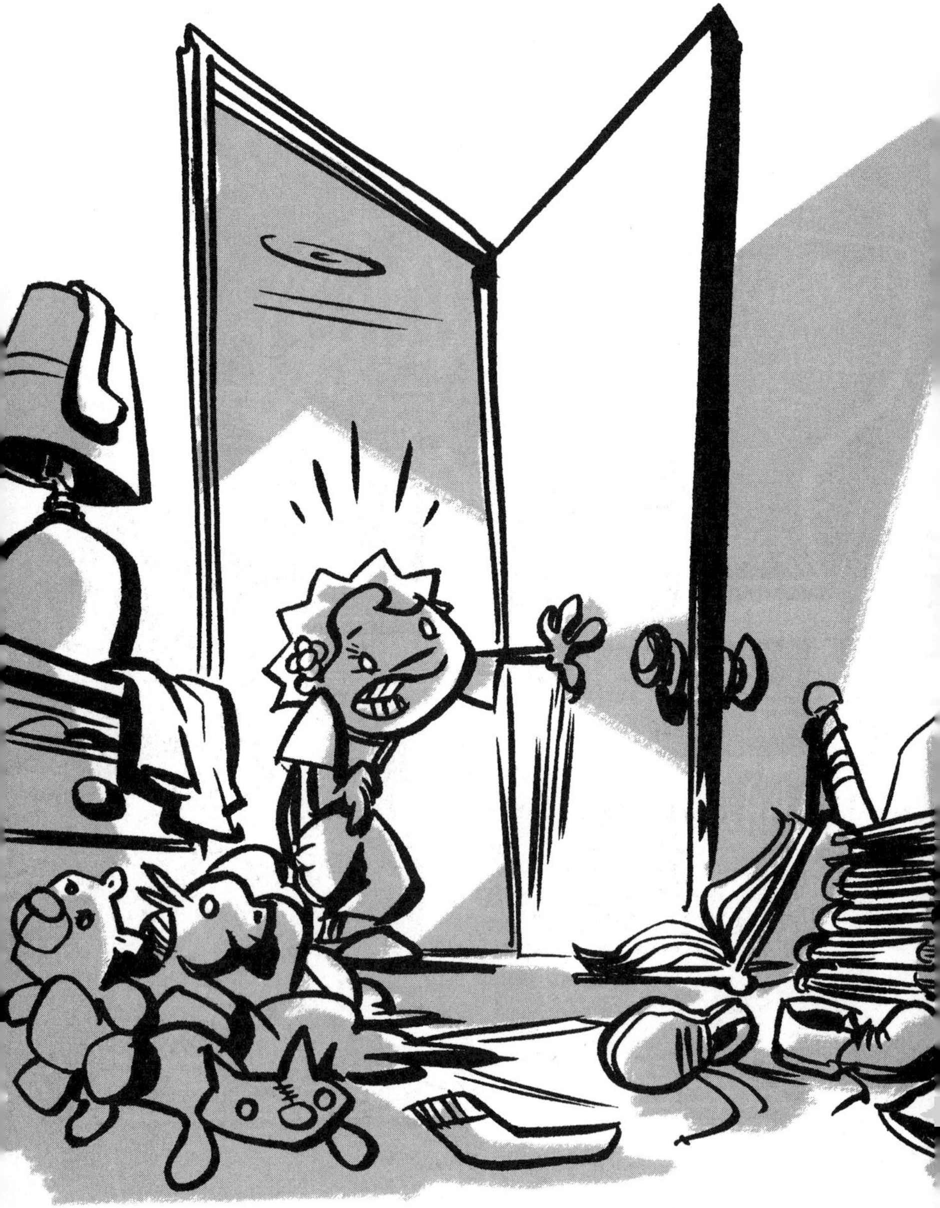

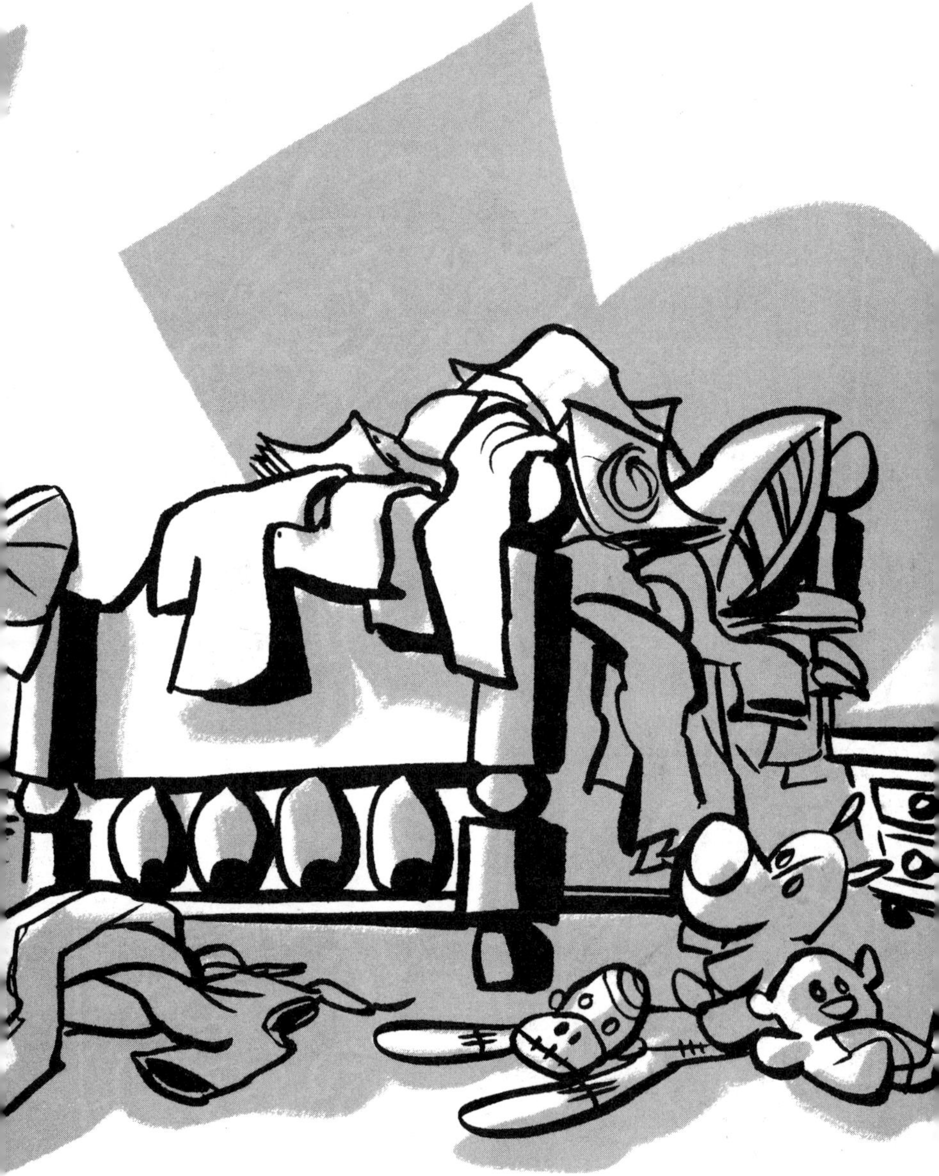

can't even see my bed! I better go pop open a jar of help," said Jo Jo. "This place needs to be *super*-clean."

She kicked aside a toy pony, which upended a giant teddy bear, which landed on a toy monkey that squealed

"HOOHOOHAW! HOOHOOHAW!"

over and over. Jo Jo ignored the mess and flipped up the edge of a throw rug. She opened the secret hatch that lay beneath.

"Hey, brine-breath!" Jo Jo shouted down the hatch. "Can you give me a hand up here?"

No answer. Jo Jo frowned. The Magic

Pickle was usually in his secret headquarters unless he was out fighting crime. Could there be some huge battle for the fate of all food raging at that moment? He hadn't mentioned anything before Jo Jo left for school that morning.

She jumped down through the hatch to investigate.

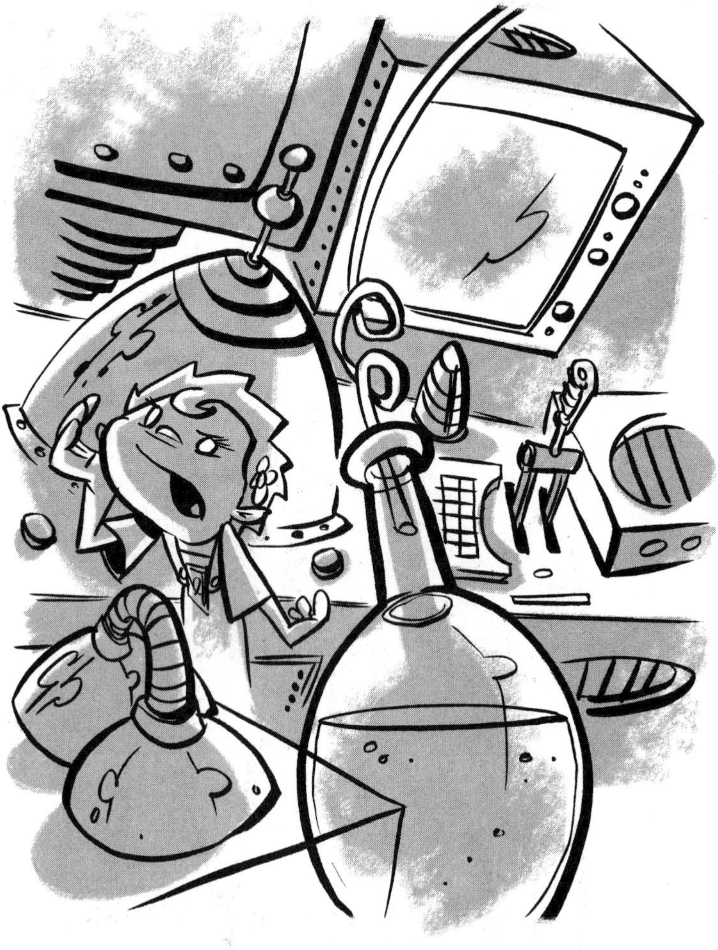

"Hello? You in here, green machine?" Jo Jo called. She glanced at the spinning gears, blinking buttons, and flickering screens on the Magic Pickle's giant Crime Computer.

"Hey, you!" a voice shouted from down the hallway. The hallway led to the cell block where the Magic Pickle kept all of his captured enemies on ice. He called it his Frozen Food Section.

"Hey, you! Peek-a-boo!" the voice called again. Jo Jo peered down the hallway. A crazy-faced piece of fruit peered back at her from behind bars.

"I overheard all that fuss, about your trip on the bus," grinned the villain. It was the Rhyming Lime. "Now you're lookin' for Greenie to help you get cleany?"

"Yeah, where'd he go?" Jo Jo asked.

"I wouldn't know," the Rhyming Lime replied.

"Wow, thanks for the help," groaned Jo Jo.

"You don't have to yelp," said the Rhyming Lime. "I've got a good plan, I'll help if I can, just get rid of your pout, grab the keys, let me out. I'll help you get tidy . . . that sound good then, all righty?"

"Heh-heh," laughed Jo Jo. "No way, pal. I know how you work. You're trying to drive me crazy with your sour rhymes!"

"Aww, come on! You're not a pawn!" the Rhyming Lime wheedled.

"Yeah, right," frowned Jo Jo.

BWUHUUHUUHU!

Jo Jo spun around and saw another villain who was blubbering behind bars. What a sad sack!

"What's the matter with you, Onion Ringer?" asked Jo Jo.

"Don't believe that crazy citrus," sobbed the Onion Ringer. "That lime may talk in rhymes, but there's no rhyme to his reason."

"Put a lid on it, both of you, before I soak you in vinegar, throw you in a jar, and put a lid on *that*!" a voice boomed.

The Magic Pickle had returned.

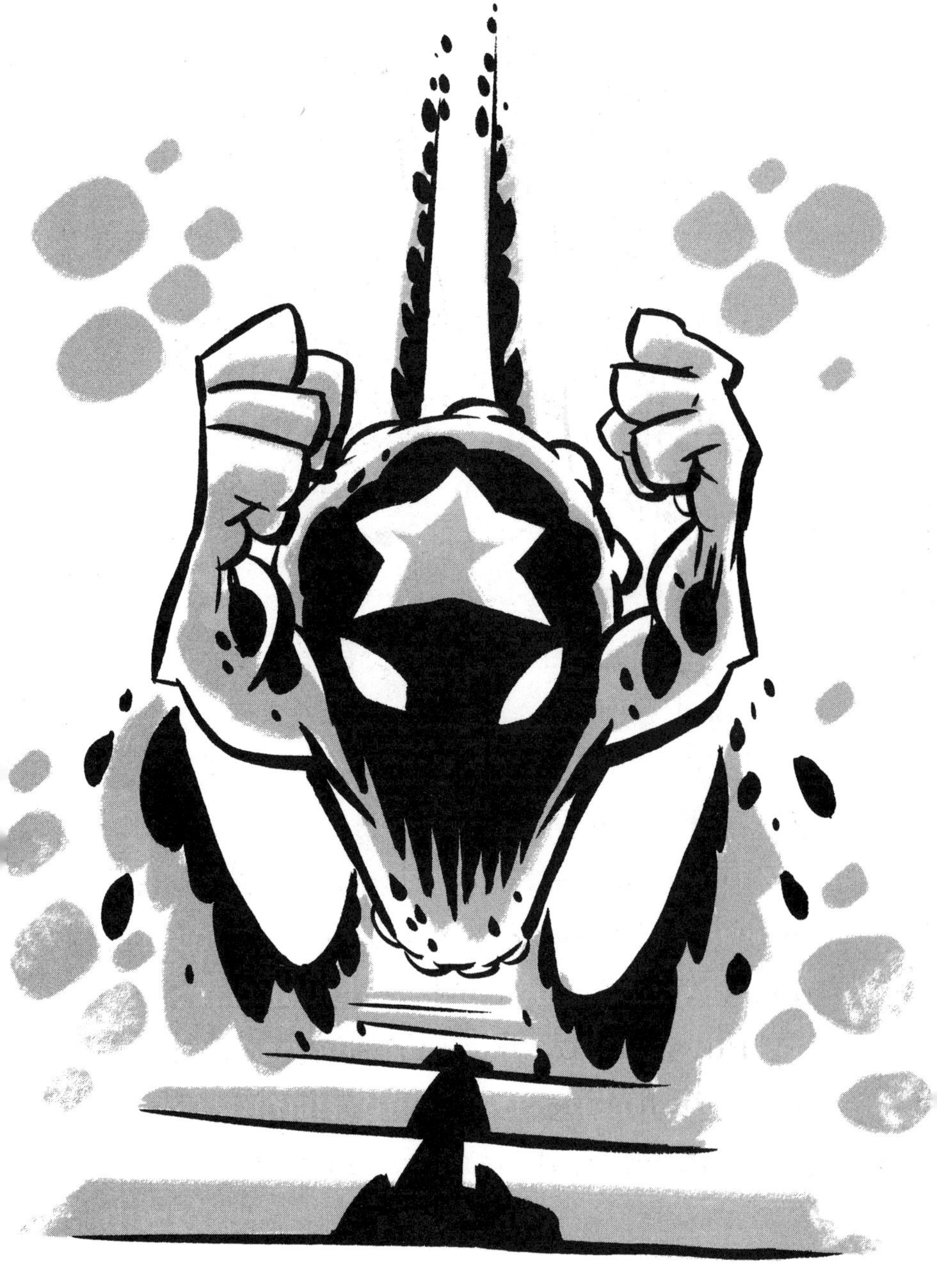

"Are these leftovers giving you a rotten time?" the Magic Pickle asked Jo Jo. He led her out of the hallway and back toward the Crime Computer. The Magic Pickle hovered over the keyboard and began typing furiously. He looked a little nervous.

"Not really," Jo Jo assured him. "I was just looking for you. I need some help cleaning my room!"

The Magic Pickle stared at her.

"I'm an agent of justice, not a maid!" he snapped and typed faster. A supermarket appeared on the screen.

"But my room has to be cleaned *super*-fast, and since you're *super*-powered, I figured you'd be the guy to ask!" Jo Jo continued.

"How fast?" asked the Magic Pickle.

"Like, before dinner!" Jo Jo answered. "Or I won't get to go on my class field trip to the zoo!"

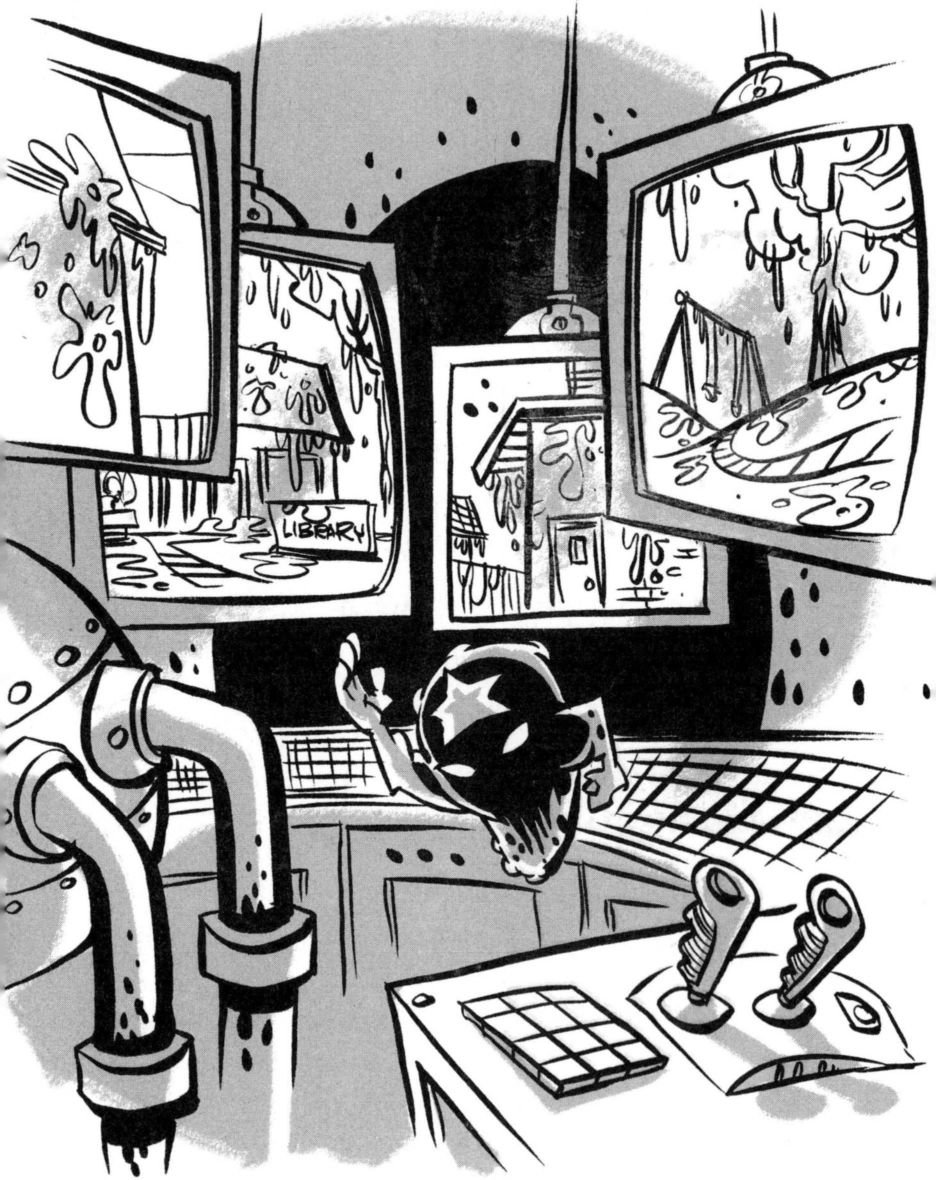
LIBRARY

Meanwhile, pictures from all over town began to pop up on the Crime Computer screen: Jo Jo's school, the library, the park. They all looked the same. Each place was littered with broken eggshells and dripping with slimy egg whites and glowing yellow yolks.

"As you can see, I've got some sticky business of my own!" the Magic Pickle pointed out.

A picture of the zoo's entrance sign suddenly popped up on a screen. It was covered in egg.

"What's with all the eggs?" asked Jo Jo. "It looks like the whole town's part of a soufflé!"

The Magic Pickle looked at Jo Jo with fear in his eye.

"I think I've created a **MONSTER!**" he cried.

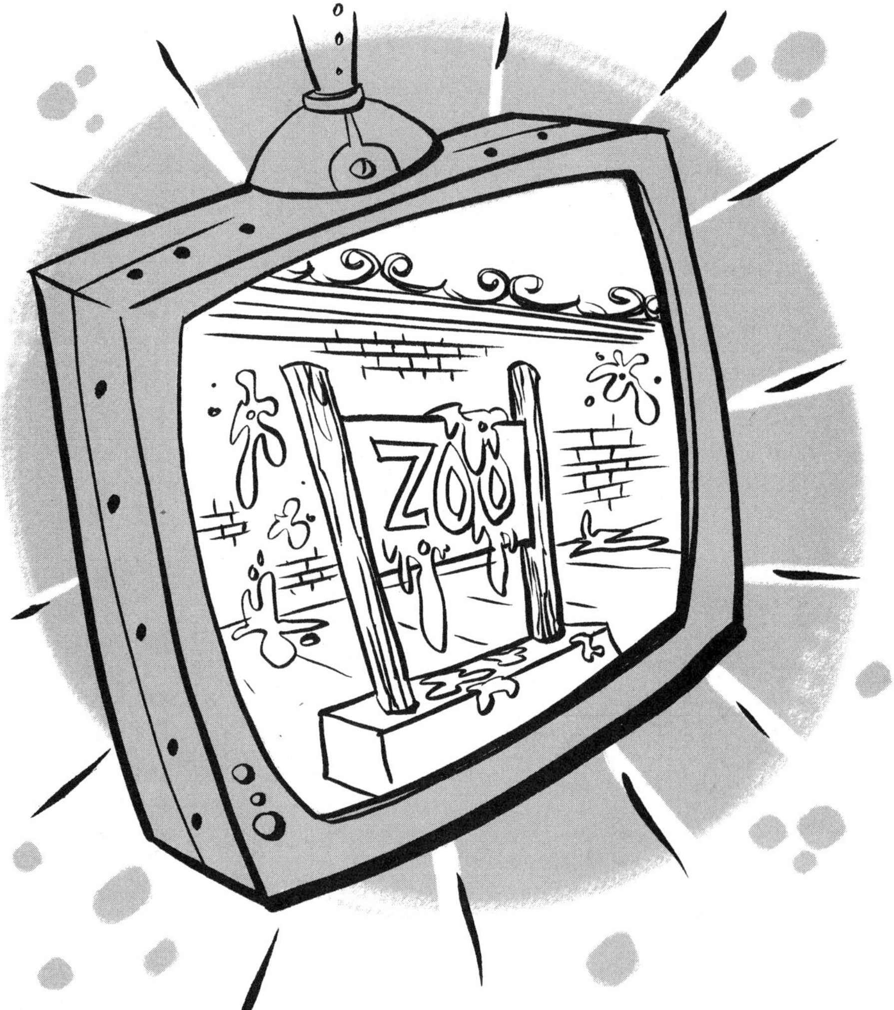
ZOO

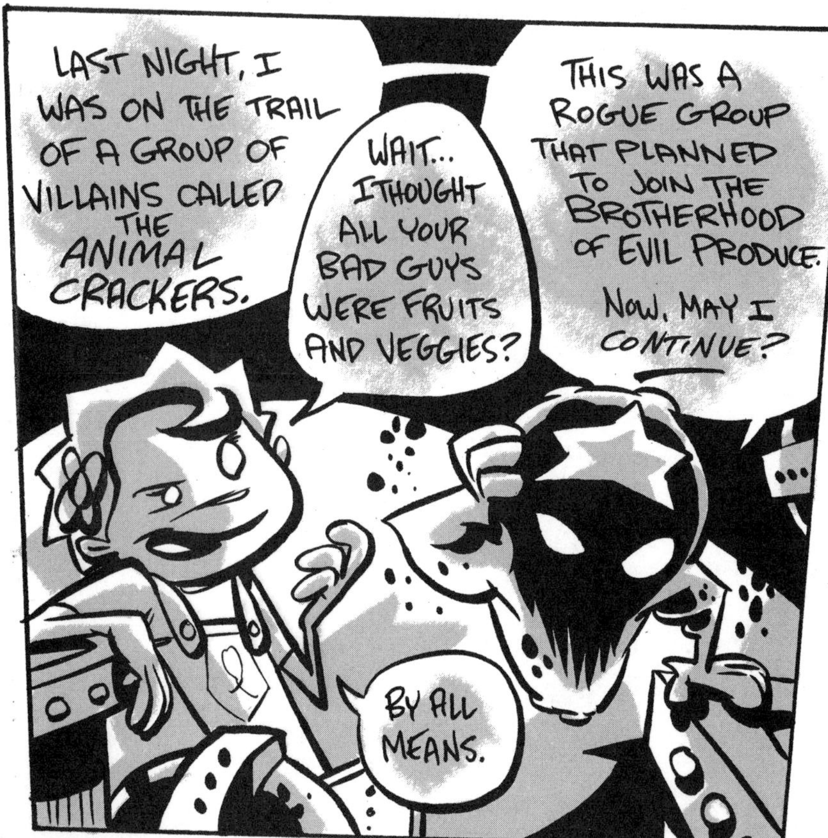
LAST NIGHT, I WAS ON THE TRAIL OF A GROUP OF VILLAINS CALLED THE ANIMAL CRACKERS.
WAIT... I THOUGHT ALL YOUR BAD GUYS WERE FRUITS AND VEGGIES?
THIS WAS A ROGUE GROUP THAT PLANNED TO JOIN THE BROTHERHOOD OF EVIL PRODUCE.
NOW, MAY I CONTINUE?
BY ALL MEANS.

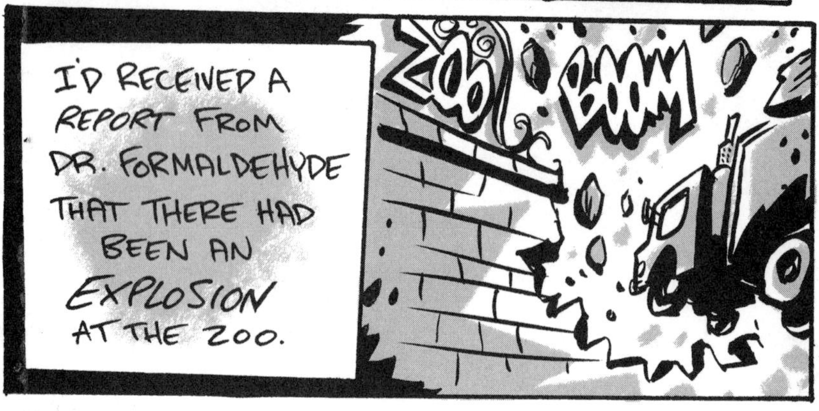
I'D RECEIVED A REPORT FROM DR. FORMALDEHYDE THAT THERE HAD BEEN AN EXPLOSION AT THE ZOO.
ZOO
BOOM

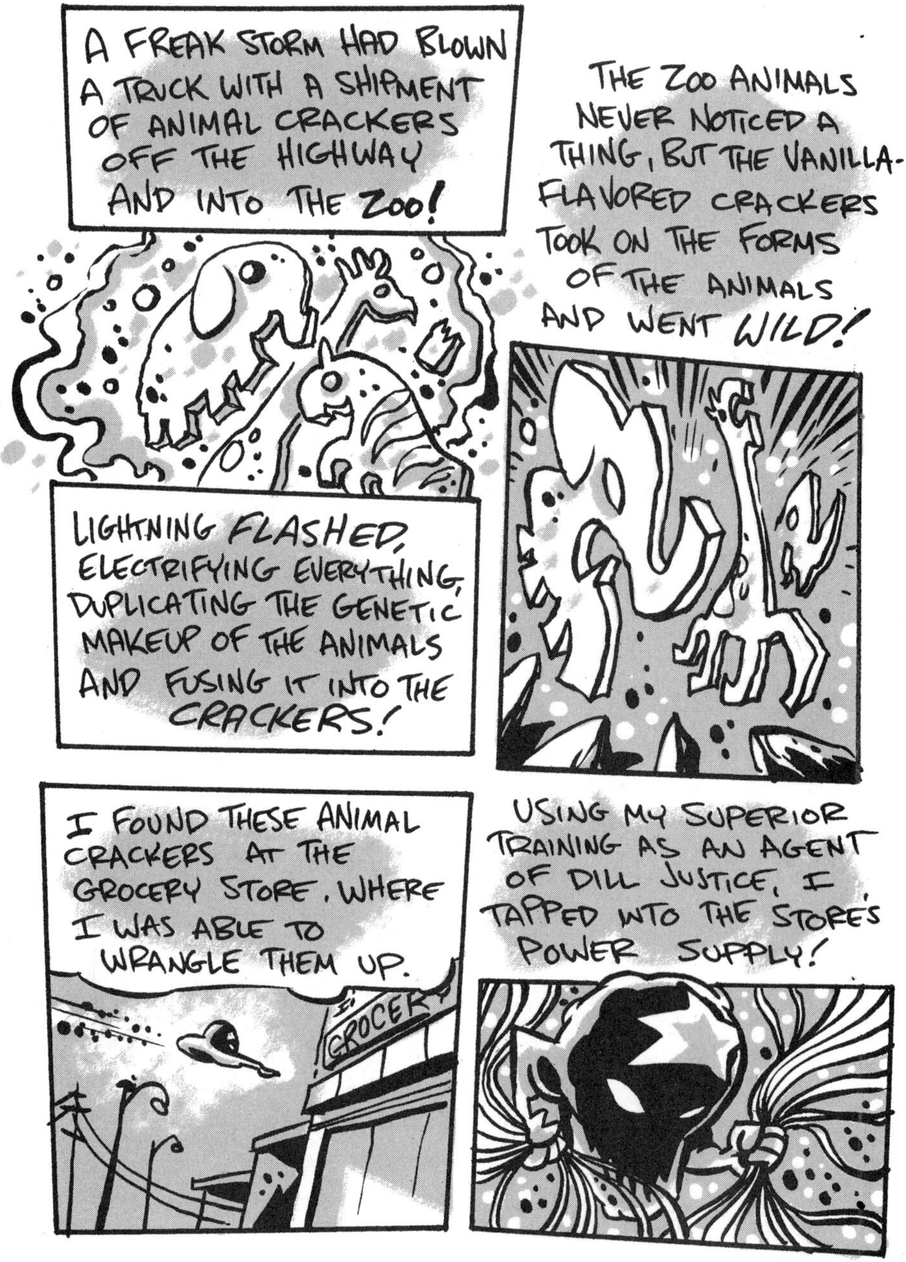
A FREAK STORM HAD BLOWN A TRUCK WITH A SHIPMENT OF ANIMAL CRACKERS OFF THE HIGHWAY AND INTO THE ZOO!
THE ZOO ANIMALS NEVER NOTICED A THING, BUT THE VANILLA-FLAVORED CRACKERS TOOK ON THE FORMS OF THE ANIMALS AND WENT WILD!
LIGHTNING FLASHED, ELECTRIFYING EVERYTHING, DUPLICATING THE GENETIC MAKEUP OF THE ANIMALS AND FUSING IT INTO THE CRACKERS!
I FOUND THESE ANIMAL CRACKERS AT THE GROCERY STORE, WHERE I WAS ABLE TO WRANGLE THEM UP.
GROCER
USING MY SUPERIOR TRAINING AS AN AGENT OF DILL JUSTICE, I TAPPED INTO THE STORE'S POWER SUPPLY!

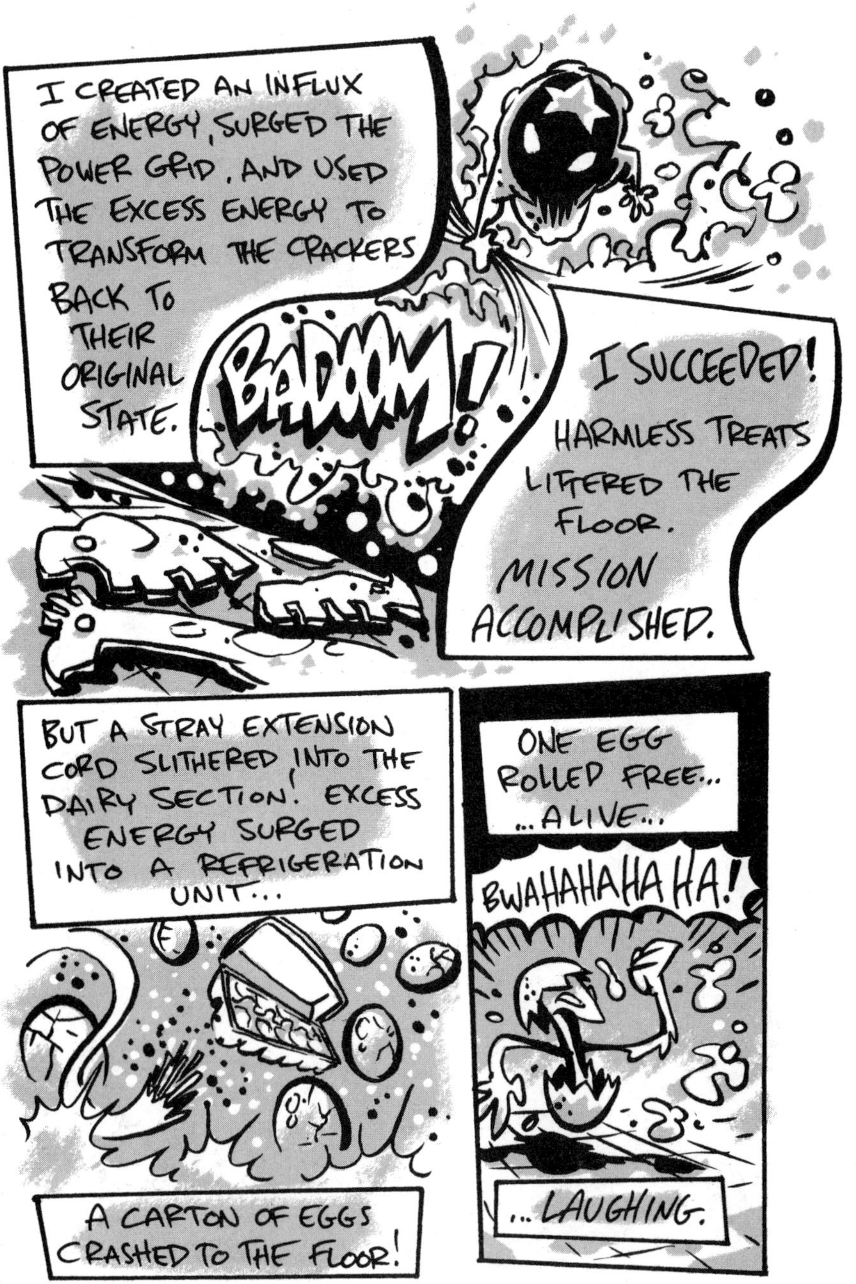
I CREATED AN INFLUX OF ENERGY, SURGED THE POWER GRID, AND USED THE EXCESS ENERGY TO TRANSFORM THE CRACKERS BACK TO THEIR ORIGINAL STATE.
BADOOM!
I SUCCEEDED!
HARMLESS TREATS LITTERED THE FLOOR.
MISSION ACCOMPLISHED.
BUT A STRAY EXTENSION CORD SLITHERED INTO THE DAIRY SECTION! EXCESS ENERGY SURGED INTO A REFRIGERATION UNIT...
A CARTON OF EGGS CRASHED TO THE FLOOR!
ONE EGG ROLLED FREE... ...ALIVE...
BWAHAHAHAHA HA!
...LAUGHING.

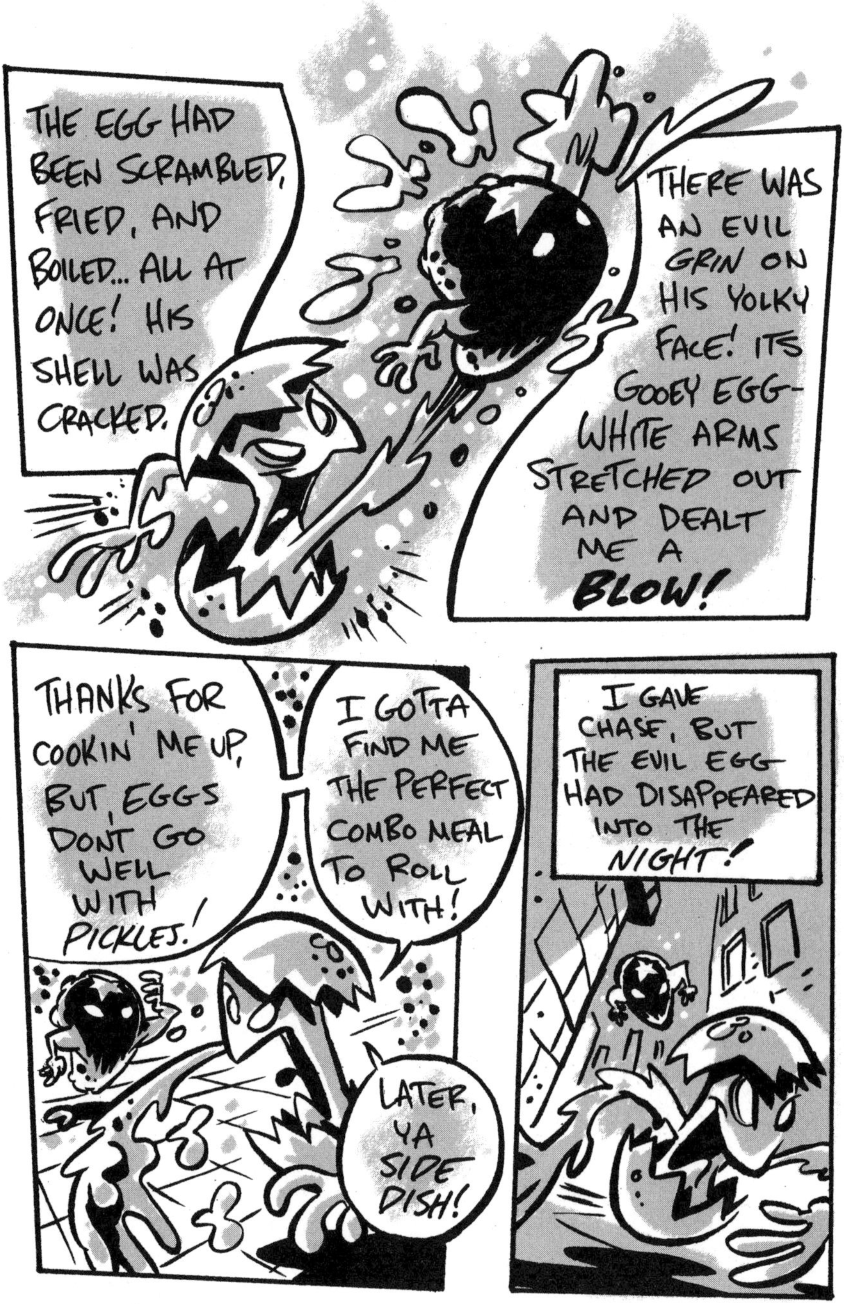
THE EGG HAD BEEN SCRAMBLED, FRIED, AND BOILED... ALL AT ONCE! HIS SHELL WAS CRACKED.
THERE WAS AN EVIL GRIN ON HIS YOLKY FACE! ITS GOOEY EGG-WHITE ARMS STRETCHED OUT AND DEALT ME A BLOW!
THANKS FOR COOKIN' ME UP, BUT EGGS DON'T GO WELL WITH PICKLES!
I GOTTA FIND ME THE PERFECT COMBO MEAL TO ROLL WITH!
LATER, YA SIDE DISH!
I GAVE CHASE, BUT THE EVIL EGG HAD DISAPPEARED INTO THE NIGHT!

Chapter 3

"What are we going to do?!" Jo Jo said, aghast.

"I fear the Egg Poacher has been sliming the entire city," said the Magic Pickle. "He mustn't be allowed to mix it up with the Brotherhood of Evil Produce. Together they could create some horrid Omelet of Evil."

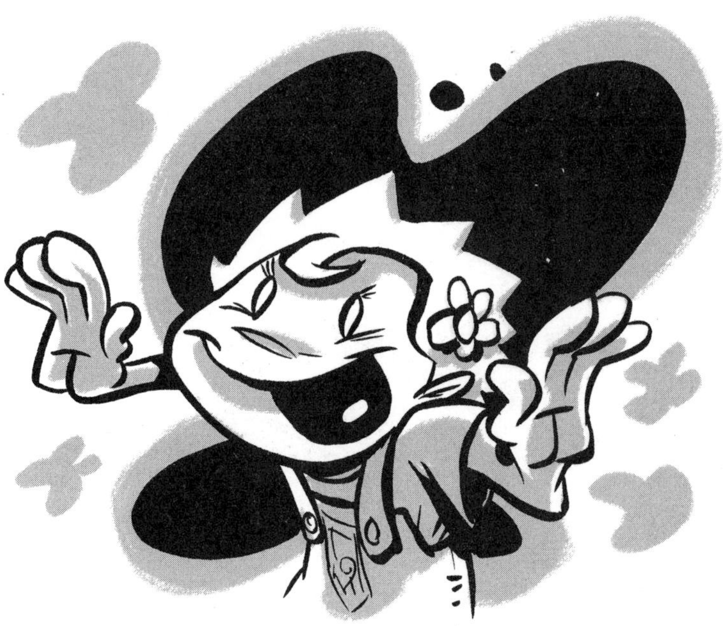

"I meant, what are we going to do about *my room*?" asked Jo Jo. "It's still a mess!"

WHHIRRRRRR!

CLICKCLICKCLICK!

"This emergency takes precedence, I'm afraid," said the Magic Pickle, searching the Crime Computer for signs of the rogue egg. Various shots of the zoo appeared on

the screens, egg slime dripping all over the different animal habitats.

"Hmmm," said the Magic Pickle. "I fear that this bad egg could be hiding in the zoo."

"Perfect!" shouted Jo Jo. "I've got the perfect plan!"

"What do you mean? Explain yourself!" demanded the Magic Pickle.

"Look, I'm supposed to go on a field trip with my class to the zoo tomorrow," Jo Jo began.

"Out of the question!" said the Magic Pickle. "Hard-boiled danger lurks there!"

"Listen! You can stow away in my lunch and I'll sneak you into the zoo so you can find this egghead!" Jo Jo explained.

The Magic Pickle pondered all this for a moment.

"Brilliant! I normally operate under cover of darkness, but your brown-bag lunch will provide me the perfect cover!" he said.

"Yeah, the only trick is, I need to clean my room before dinner or my mom won't sign my permission slip to let me even go to the zoo!" Jo Jo reminded him. "Which is why I need your—HEY!"

Jo Jo watched wide-eyed as the Magic Pickle zoomed through the hatch into her bedroom. Jo Jo scrambled up.

"Hey, wait up! I need your help to clean my—"

Jo Jo crawled up into her bedroom where the Magic Pickle hovered, arms crossed, proud.

The room was spotless!

The clothes were hung up, the dirty laundry stowed in the laundry basket, her teddy was propped up on her pillows, and her baseball cap hung on her bedpost.

"HOOHOOHAW! HOOHOOHAW!"

The toy monkey was still going; the ON button was stuck.

Magic Pickle swooped down, turned it over, and quickly removed the batteries.

"You did it all! You're the BEST!" Jo Jo squealed.

"There's still your evening meal to deal with," said the Magic Pickle. "Clean your dinner plate and get that permission slip signed! We've got an egg to crack!"

Chapter 4

The school bus rolled to a stop outside the tall, iron gates of the zoo. All the students ran for the entrance. Everyone was excited to be out of the classroom and in the open air! Who knew what kind of crazy animals they'd see today, and not in a book; they were going to see the real thing!

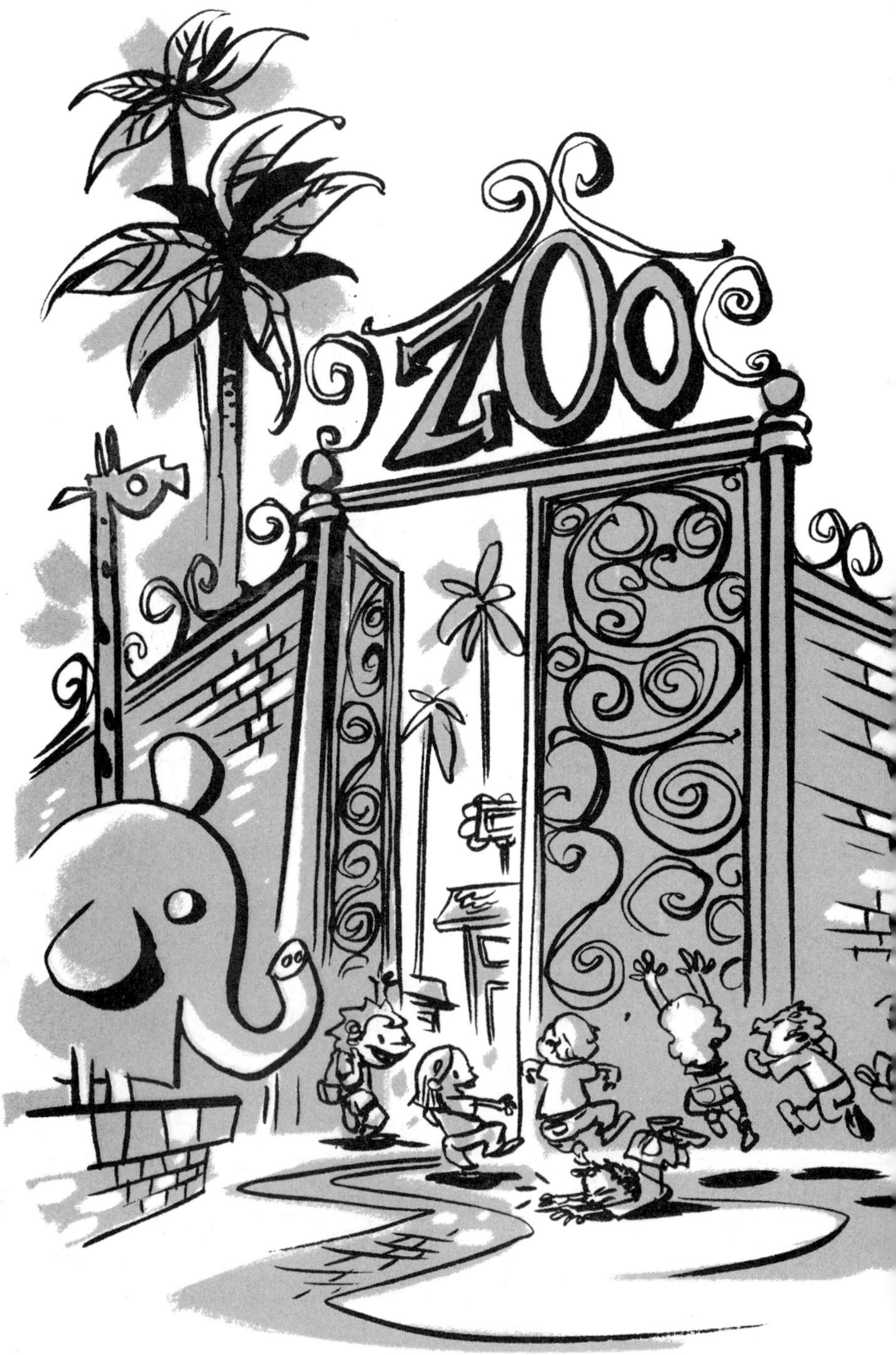
ZOO

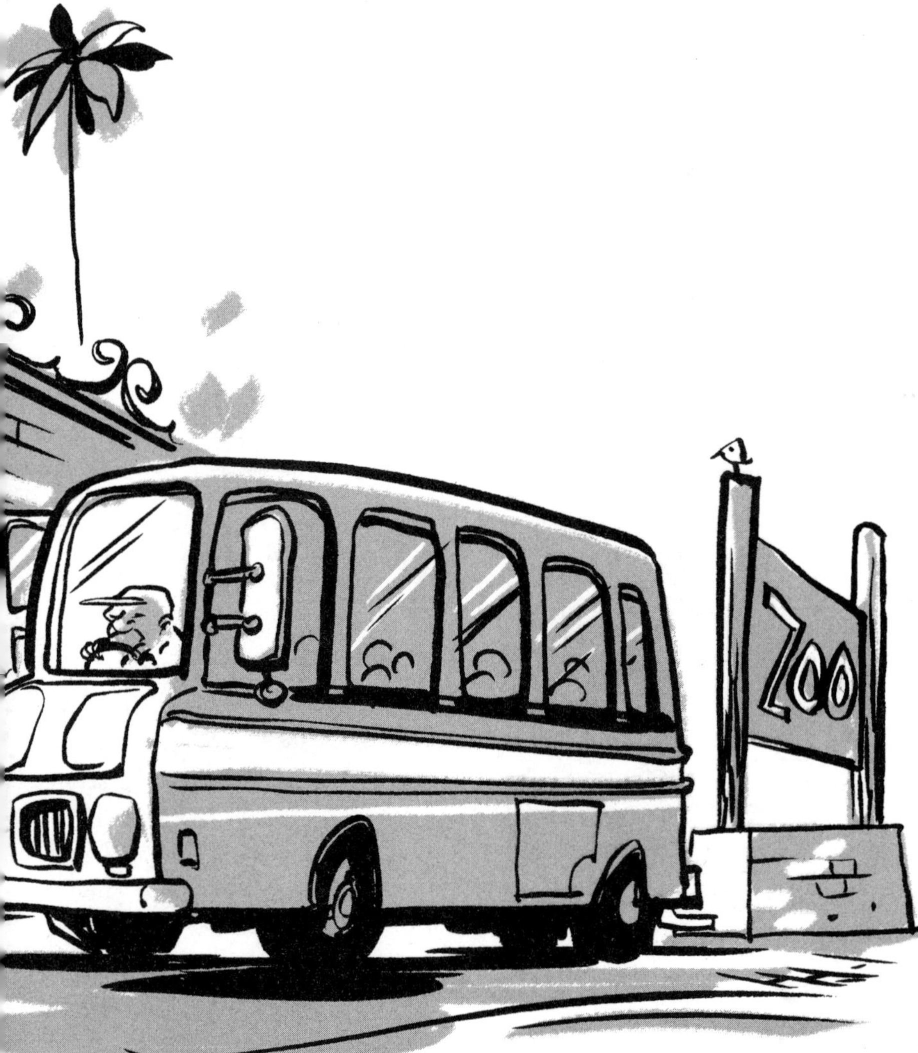
ZOO

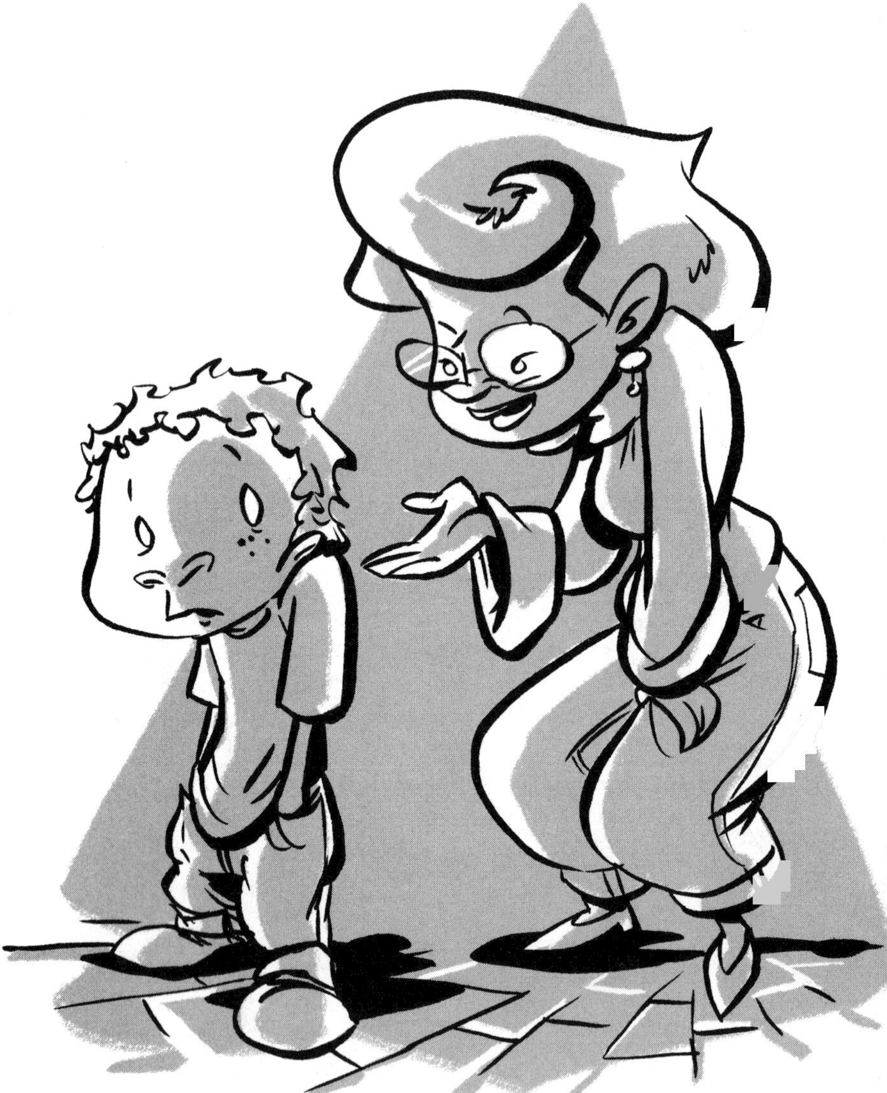

Jo Jo's teacher, Miss Emilyek, gathered the class into a tight group for an announcement.

"I know this is all very exciting, but we need to stay together so no one gets lost. We're using the 'buddy system' today, so everyone needs a partner," Miss Emilyek explained.

Jo Jo and Ellen grabbed hands right away.

"And now for your assignment . . ." said Miss Emilyek.

"AWWW," the class groaned.

Miss Emilyek ignored the griping and continued. "Each team of 'buddies' must gather five facts while at the zoo today. These five facts must be about five different animals. The facts can be about what the animals eat, how they raise their young, where they live—"

"They live in the zoo!" shouted Mikey. He looked pleased with himself.

HAHAHAHA!!!

Everyone giggled. Now Mikey looked bewildered.

"Well, they do!" Mikey assured his classmates, very seriously.

"I want to know where the animals live in their *natural habitats*, Mikey," said Miss Emilyek. "For instance, a bear lives in the forest, and a tiger lives in the jungle."

Jo Jo rolled her eyes at Mikey with a smile. He giggled back nervously.

"Now, remember, this is a *class* trip, so stay together, class," finished Miss Emilyek. "And everyone be on their best behavior, please. The zoo has had some recent incidents of eggs being thrown about."

"Someone egged the zoo?" asked Mikey.

"They've cleaned it up, I think," Miss Emilyek answered. "Just mind your manners and let's go, everyone."

"Psst, Jo Jo. I gotta go to the bathroom,"

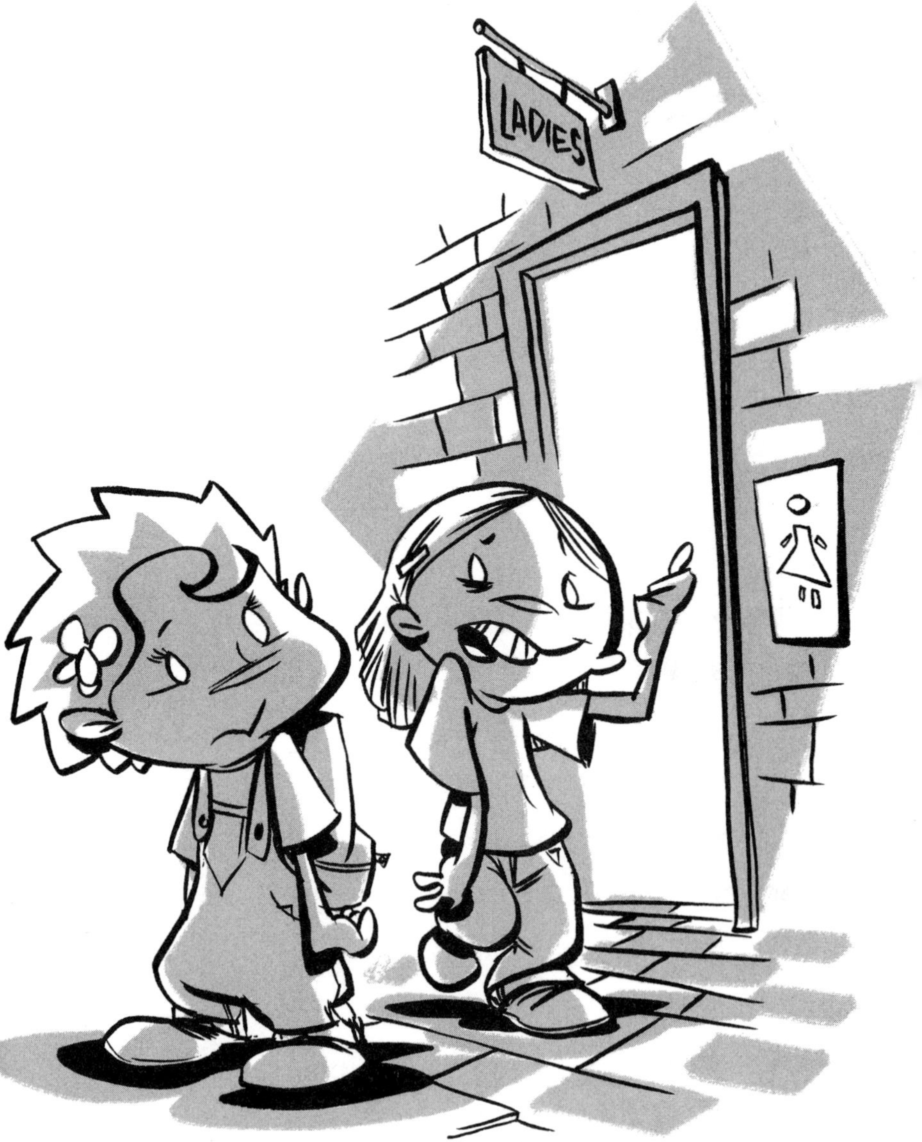
LADIES

Ellen whispered. She pointed to a nearby sign. "Wait for me," she said and ran in.

Miss Emilyek and the class had already marched off.

Jo Jo shrugged. What could she do? Ellen was her buddy. "Hold on, Ellen," she said. "I'll come, too.

The two girls disappeared into the bathroom. But by the time they came out, their class had disappeared!

Jo Jo and Ellen stared at the crossroads sign. Reptiles? Elephants? Monkeys? Birds? Which way should they go?

"I say we hit the monkeys," said Ellen. "That's probably where the class went first."

Jo Jo's backpack began to shift against her shoulder. She peeked over her shoulder to adjust it. Two glowing yellow eyes and a blue star flashed from under the top flap of her pack.

GASP!

Jo Jo had almost forgotten that she had the Magic Pickle stowed away in her backpack!

"What's wrong?" asked Ellen, still looking at the signs. "Monkeys are funny!"

"Uh, nothing . . . I thought I forgot my lunch, that's all, but it's in my backpack," Jo Jo answered quickly. She peeked back

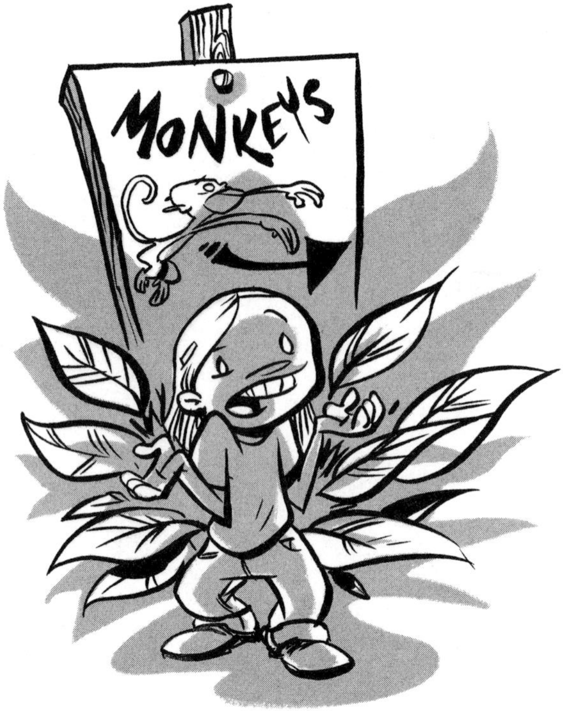
MONKEYS

again and saw that the Magic Pickle was trying to get a better view of the zoo from beneath the flap of the backpack.

"Okay, fine," said Ellen. "Then let's head for the Monkey House."

"Remember, we're after a bad egg," the Magic Pickle whispered to Jo Jo. "Look for animals that might lay eggs. Our villain may try to hide out in their nest."

Jo Jo looked back at Ellen, who was a few steps ahead. Jo Jo called her back.

"Wait! If the class is going to hit the monkeys first," Jo Jo reasoned, "why don't we go off and check out some animals everyone else might miss. We can catch up later, before Miss Emilyek even notices we're gone."

"Like, what animals?" wondered Ellen.

"Ummm . . . maybe like, the scary animals, like, ummm—" Jo Jo was stuck. She couldn't think of where there might be eggs in a zoo. "Like, the flamingos?"

"*Flamingos!*" giggled Ellen. "The only thing scary about flamingos is that they might fall over, standing on one leg all the time!" She laughed out loud.

"Heh, yeah, good one," giggled Jo Jo nervously.

"Reptiles lay eggs," said the Magic Pickle aloud. He sounded urgent.

Ellen looked up at Jo Jo with wide eyes.

"Ummm, OK," said Ellen. "I never really thought about it. That's a weird fact we can add to our list if it's true. We can hit the Reptile House if you want to find out, though I think reptiles are pretty scary. By the way, do you have a cold? You sound so hoarse."

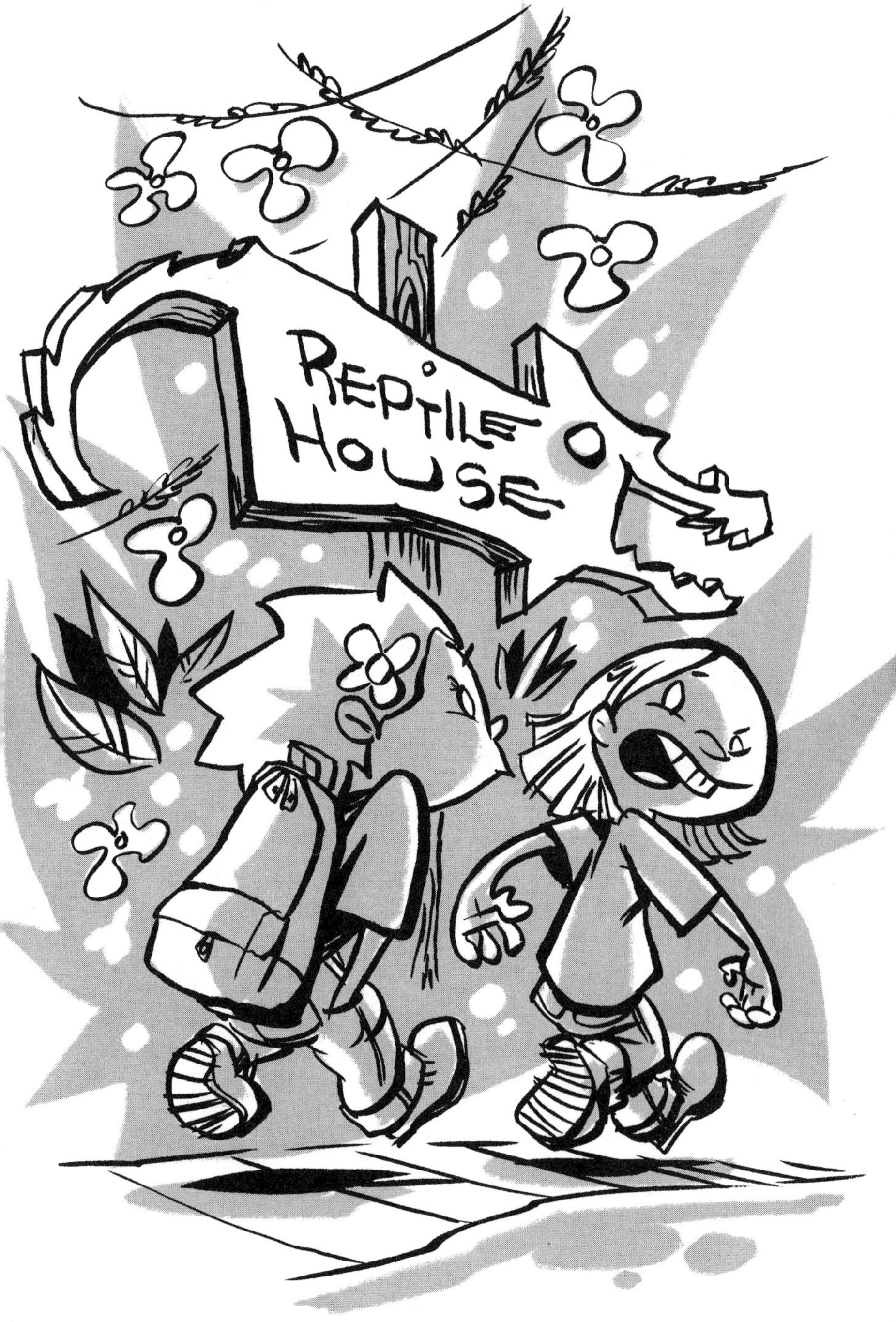
REPTILE HOUSE

"I'm fine. Let's go," Jo Jo said nervously.

Jo Jo and Ellen walked quickly toward the Reptile House. Jo Jo tightened the flap of her backpack as they walked, pushing the Magic Pickle down. He squashed up

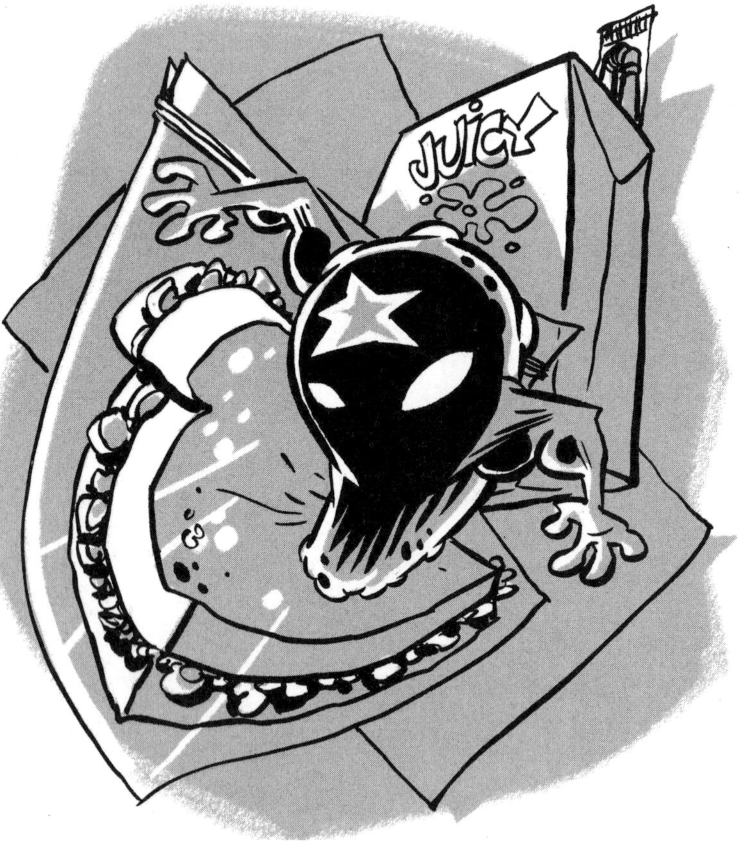
JUICY

against the egg salad sandwich her mother had packed in her lunch.

"That's all I need, more eggs," groaned the Magic Pickle.

"You better keep your voice down or someone will discover you," Jo Jo whispered over her shoulder. Ellen turned toward Jo Jo.

"I didn't even say anything!" Ellen said. "And I don't think anyone will see us. Most of the class headed toward the elephants, I think."

"Hey, look, we're here!" Jo Jo said quickly, changing the subject.

The Reptile House looked like a big cave lined with glass habitats. Each glass habitat held a different reptile. The girls walked past spiny iguanas and stopped in front of a huge monitor lizard.

"Hey, this one's funny," said Ellen, pointing at the long lizard. "The sign says he's a boy, but he's called a 'joanna.'

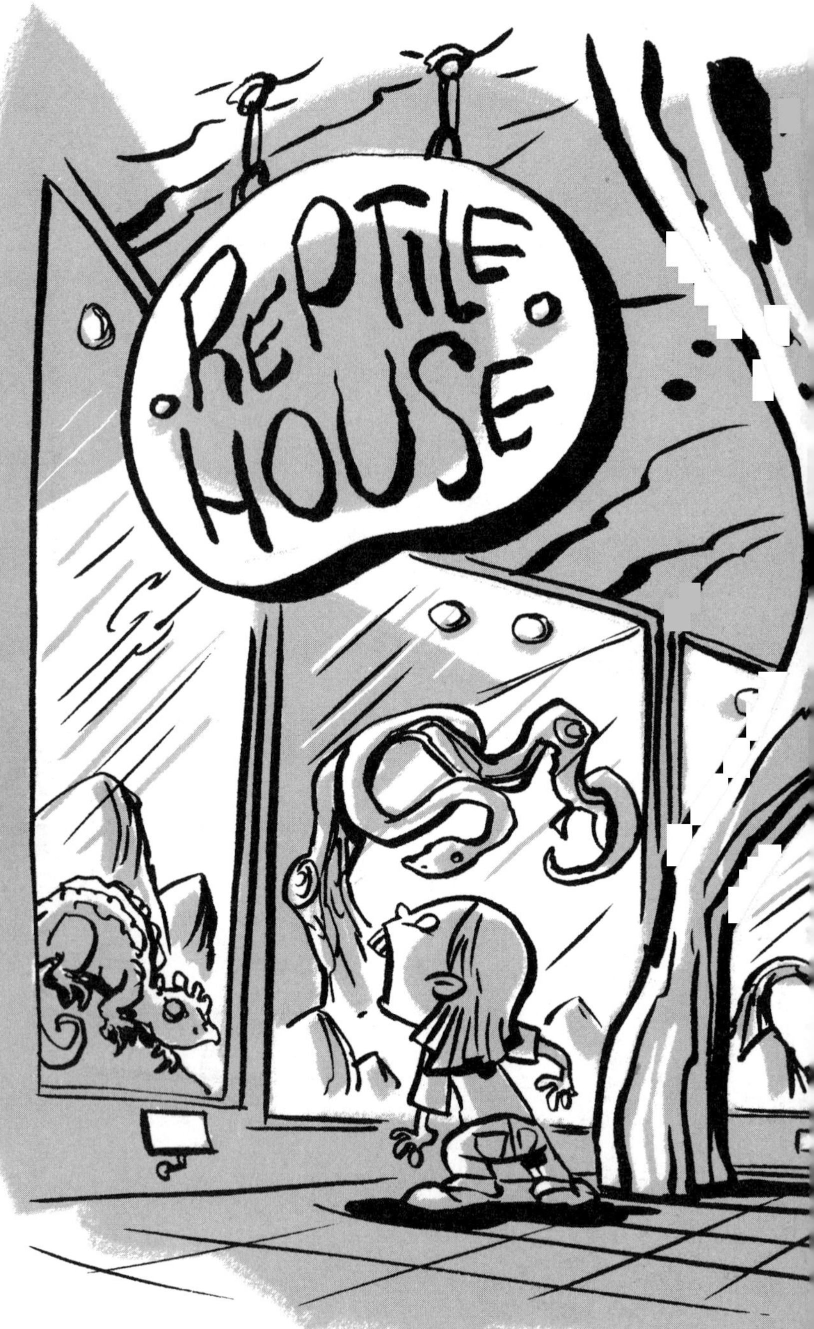
REPTILE HOUSE

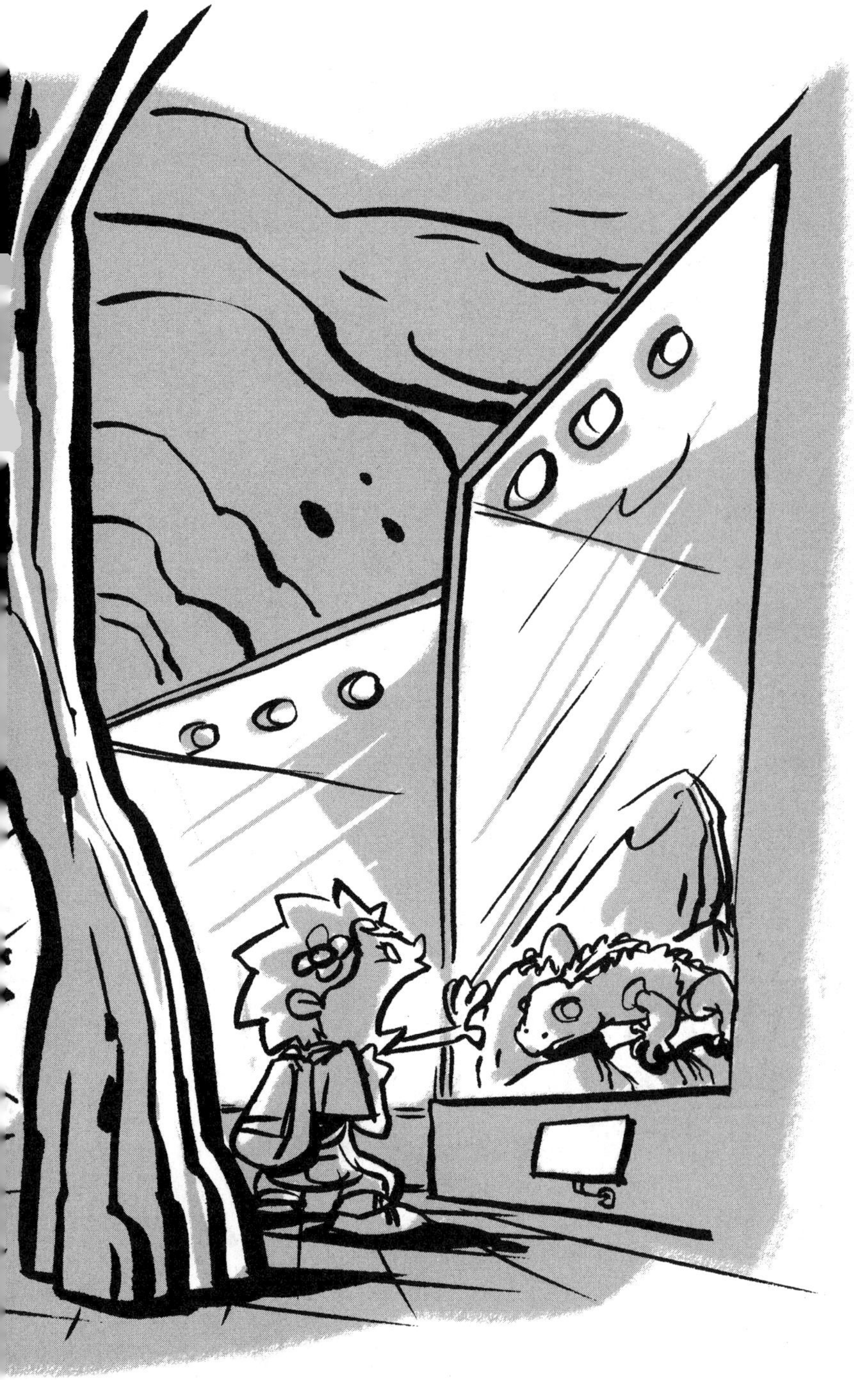

I thought that was a girl's name! Maybe because it's spelled with a G?"

"The G in *goanna* is a 'hard G,'" said a zookeeper who had stepped up behind them. "It's a fun word to say. Some people think that the word comes from *iguana*, which also has a hard G sound."

"Hey, write that down," Ellen told Jo Jo. "That's a good fact!"

Jo Jo pulled out a small pad of paper and jotted down their notes. She looked up at the zookeeper. "How do you spell . . ."

GULP!

Jo Jo leaped back in shock.

"Boy, you're jumpy today," giggled Ellen.

"She's got a huge snake on her shoulders!" cried Jo Jo. She pointed to the zookeeper.

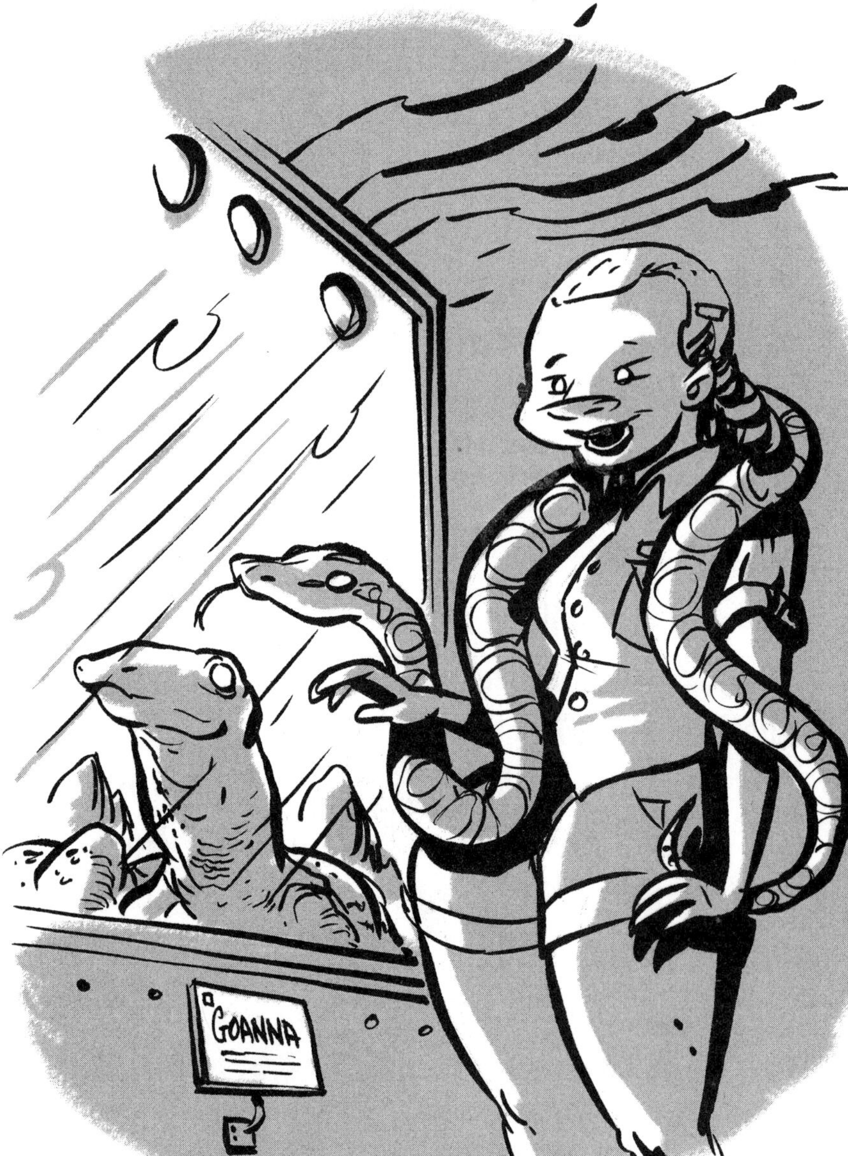
GOANNA

Ellen jumped behind Jo Jo. Sure enough, a gigantic boa constrictor twisted its head in their direction, its body draped on the zookeeper's neck. The girls hadn't noticed the snake at first, because it blended in with the zookeeper's tan outfit. The zookeeper chuckled.

"This guy's gentle, no worries," she said. "He likes to greet visitors. You can pet him if you like."

Jo Jo and Ellen each moved a shaky hand toward the boa. They stroked its brown and black scales.

"He's smooth!" said Ellen. "I like him!"

"Could you tell us about your boa?" Jo Jo asked. "We need facts for our school report." She had her pad of paper ready.

"Well, snakes like this boa constrictor are born from eggs, and they can grow to be pretty big."

"Did you say *eggs*?" asked Jo Jo.

"Hey, you were right!" Ellen said to her.

"Yep," said the zookeeper. "Most snakes, like most reptiles, lay eggs. Some snakes even *eat* eggs and small rodents and birds—"

"They *eat* eggs, too?!" asked Ellen. She wanted to get her facts straight.

"Some do, like the egg eater over there." The zookeeper pointed to a brown-spotted

snake asleep in a glass habitat nearby. "He's a *Dasypeltis scabra*. That's his fancy scientific name."

Jo Jo wrote the name down. Ellen grabbed her arm.

"All right, enough with the cold-blooded egg suckers; let's find something with fur," she said. Ellen dragged Jo Jo out of the Reptile House. The zookeeper chuckled and waved good-bye. The boa flicked its tongue at them.

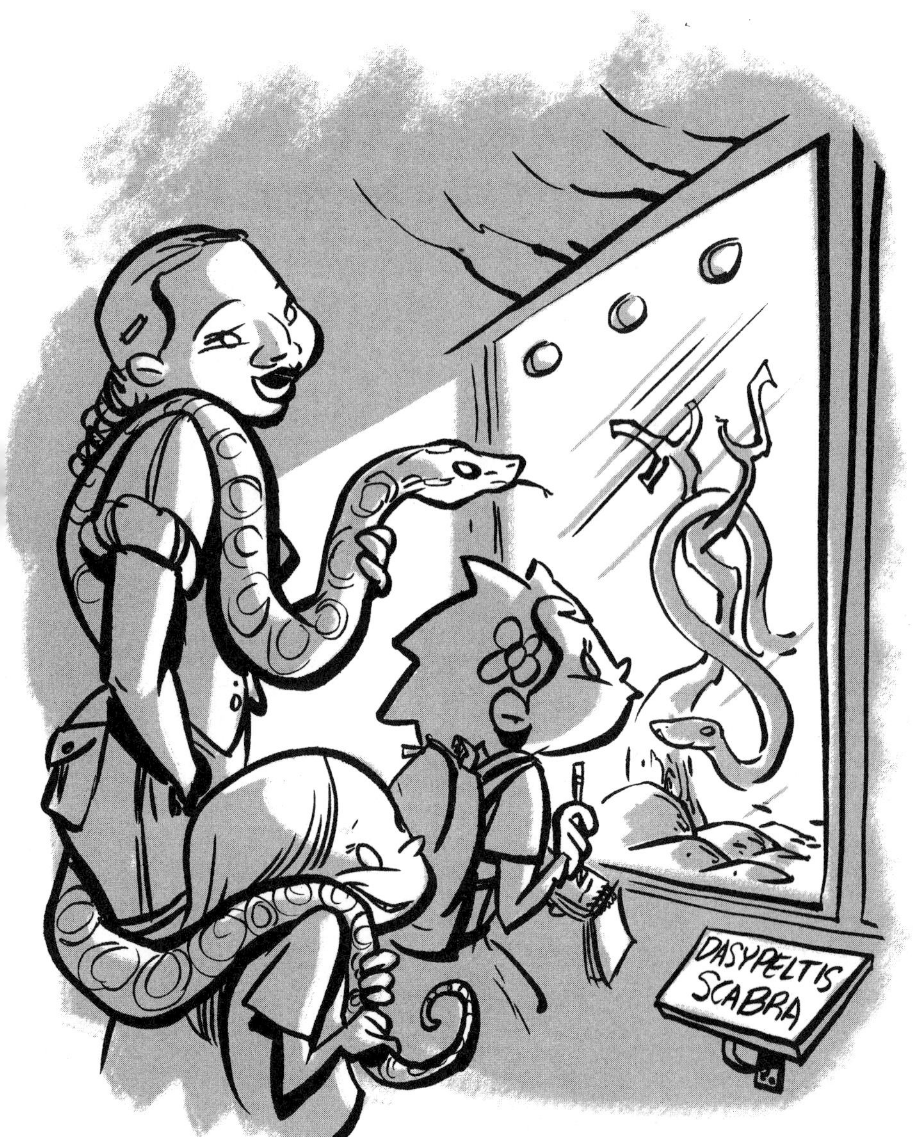
DASYPELTIS
SCABRA

Chapter 5

Ellen and Jo Jo stopped a few feet away from the Reptile House.

"Whoa!" gasped Ellen. "Check this guy out!"

A gorilla sat on a big rock, just past some bushes lining the walkway. The gorilla stared at the girls blankly. A string of slimy goo dripped from the tree branches over

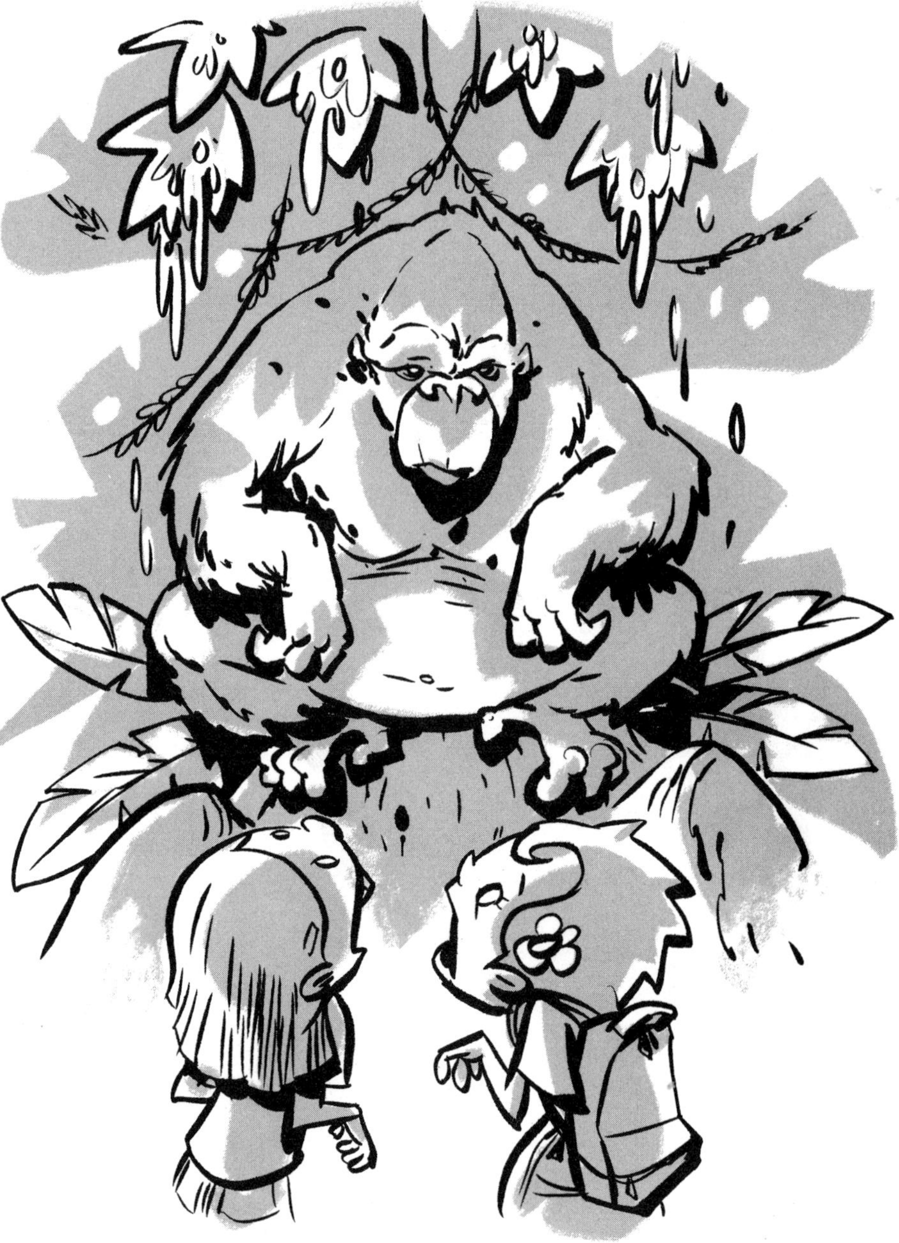

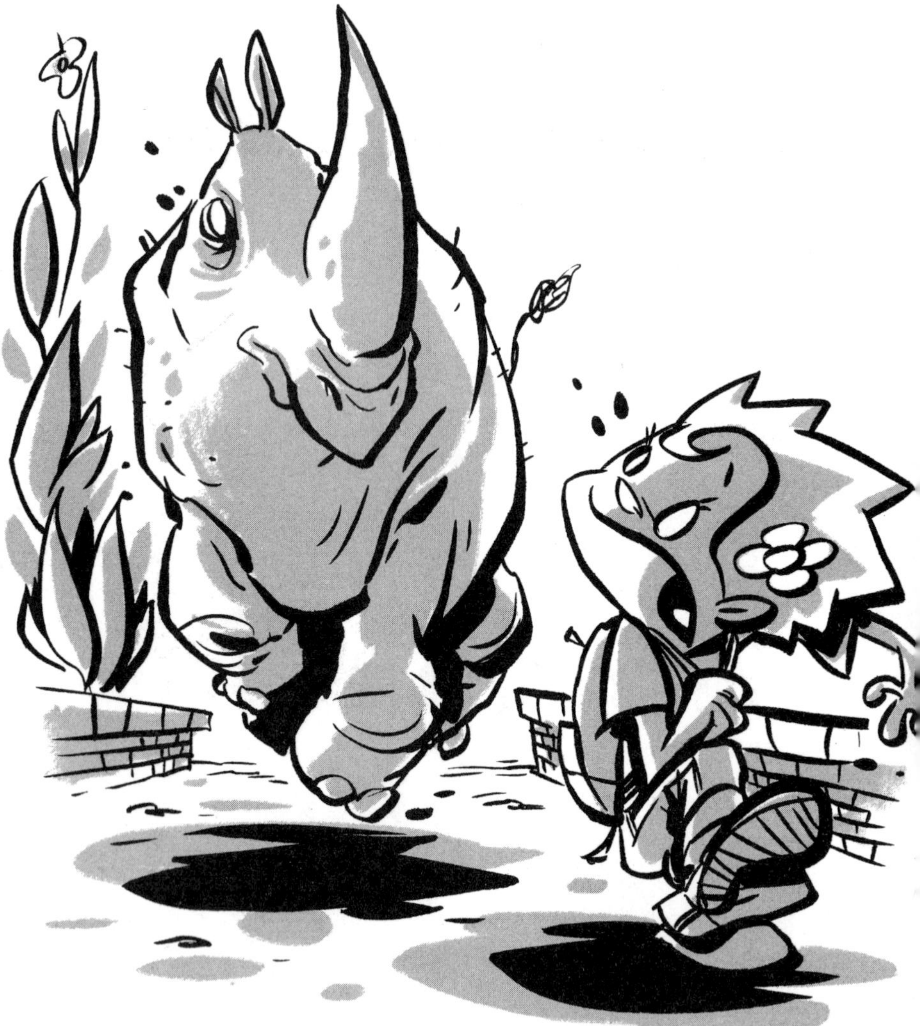

the animal's head.

"That big ape's so close!" said Jo Jo. "I can see up his nose!"

BOOM BOOM BOOM!!!

A rhino stomped down the sidewalk, headed right toward them.

"Yikes!" yelped Jo Jo. She grabbed Ellen and pulled her down behind a bench. They watched in horror as the rhino walked away.

"I never heard of free-range rhinos!" whispered Ellen.

CRREEAAAK!

Jo Jo and Ellen whipped their heads around. A tall, barnlike door swung freely. A towering giraffe stepped out past them, followed by another. Gooey raw egg dripped from the top of the giraffe house.

FFRREEEAAAWWWPP!

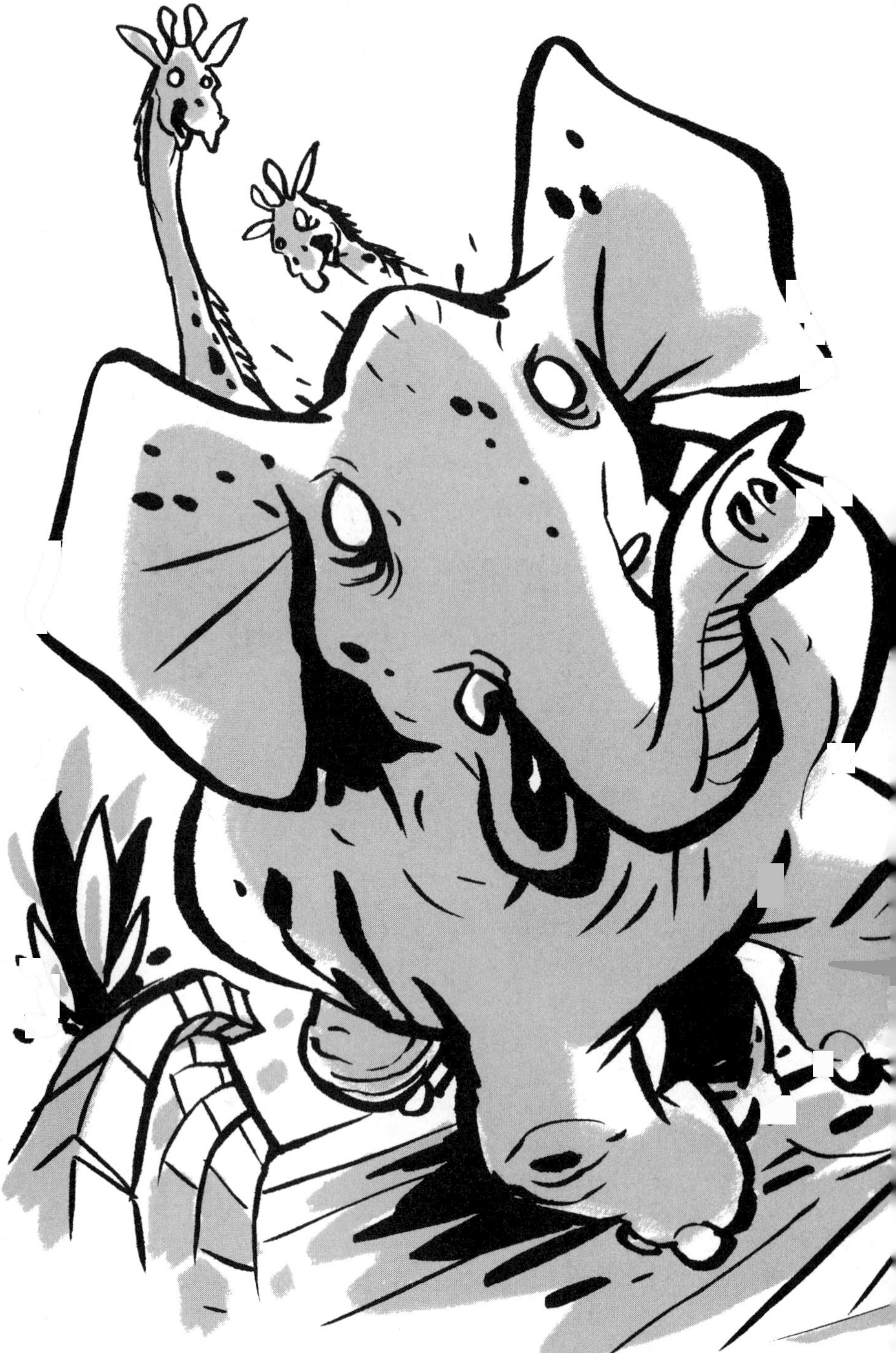

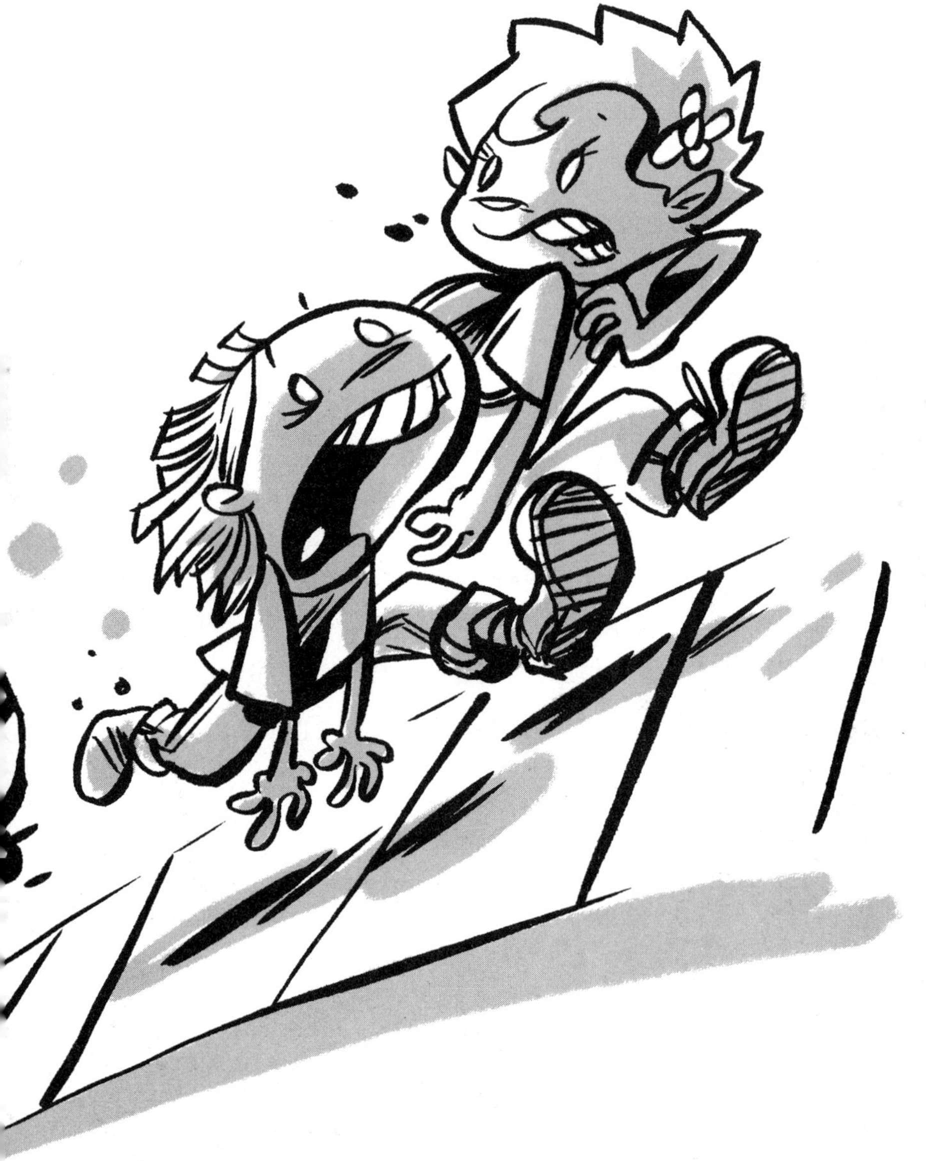

An elephant trumpeted as it lumbered toward them.

AAAIIIGGGHHHH!!!

Ellen screamed. The elephant flapped its ears, startled by Ellen's sudden squeal. Jo Jo dove back under the bench, reaching for Ellen's sleeve.

Too late! The elephant charged!

Ellen jumped up onto the back of the bench; her sleeve slipped out of Jo Jo's grasp. Ellen leaped to a low tree branch and worked her way up the tree. She had never climbed so fast in her life! When she got to a big overhanging branch, she inched down onto the roof of the Reptile House, panting.

Ellen looked to her side and saw a meerkat sitting on its haunches, anxiously surveying the chaos below.

"Aren't you supposed to be a burrowing ground animal?" she said to the small

mammal. The meerkat looked around nervously, then ducked as a monkey swung overhead and smacked right into Ellen. The girl screamed.

AAAIIIGGGHHH!!!

Below, Jo Jo ducked under the bench as rampaging zoo animals stormed past. The

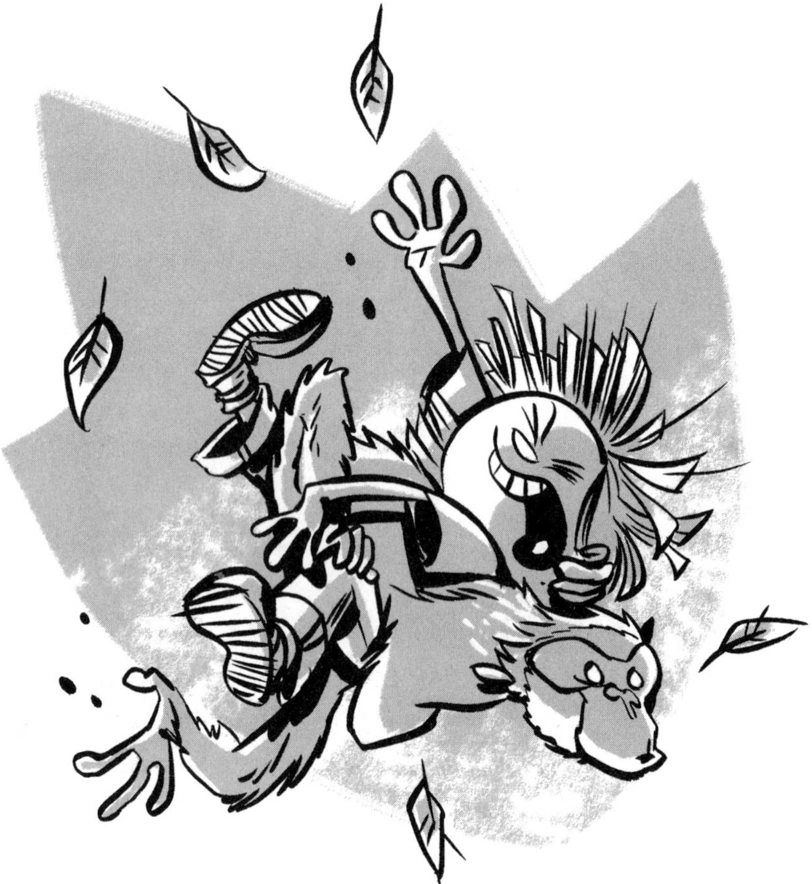

Magic Pickle shot out of her backpack in a flash of green.

"Stay down!" the Magic Pickle ordered Jo Jo. "I'll assess the situation and report back!"

"Whatever!" cried Jo Jo. "Just hurry

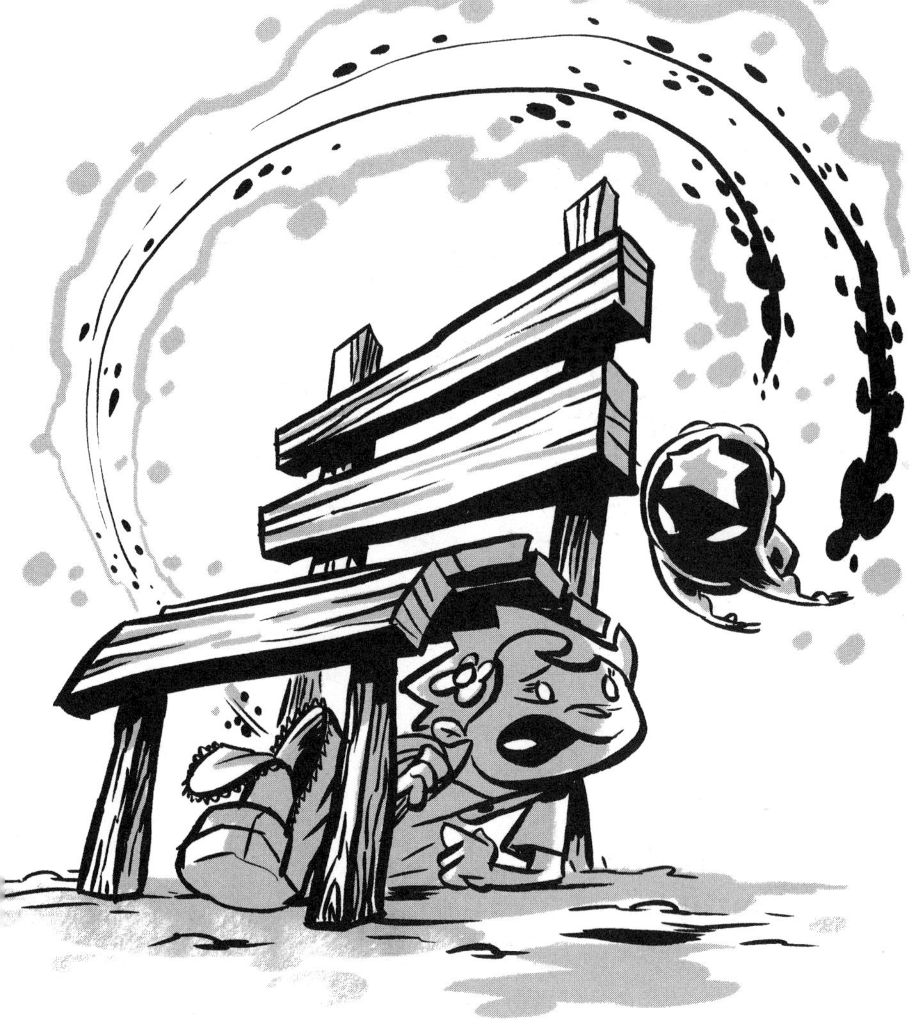

up! Forget the assessing; how about some superhero action! Whoa!"

An alligator twisted past her in a hurry.

"Try not to get eaten!" the Magic Pickle shouted.

"Look who's talking!" Jo Jo yelled. "You're the flying vegetable!"

The Magic Pickle zoomed off into the depths of the zoo.

Jo Jo went in search of Ellen.

Chapter 6

The Magic Pickle shredded through the netting that covered the gibbon monkey habitat. He hovered down through branches and leaves, glancing left and right for any sign of the Egg Poacher.

Three gibbon monkeys huddled on a branch.

"Greetings, long-armed simians," the

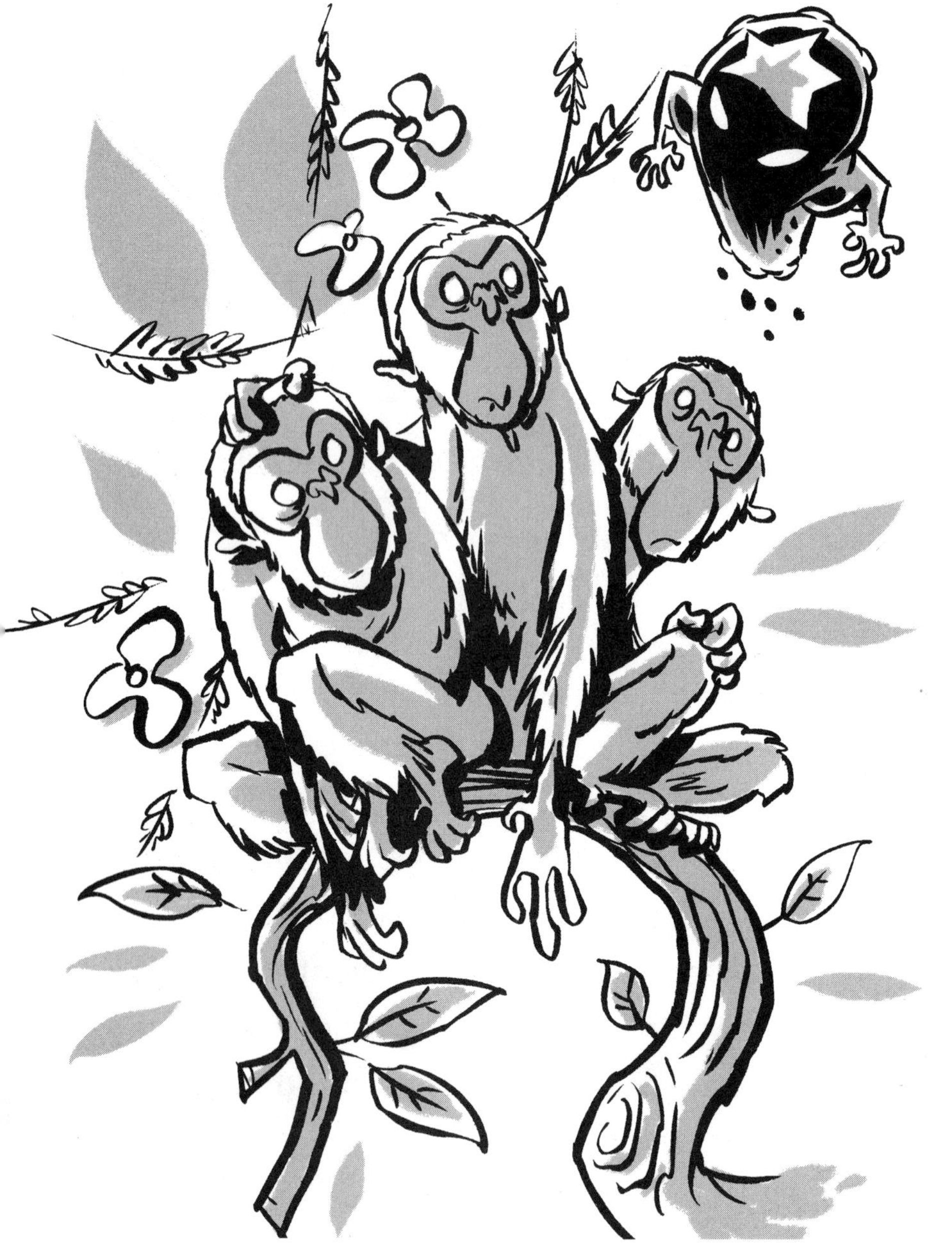

Magic Pickle said as he approached the monkeys. "I'm in search of—"

SQUAWK! SQUAWK!

The gibbons cut him off. They started throwing sticks and leaves at their food bowl on the ground.

SMACK! SMACK! SMACK!

Below them, the Egg Poacher was attacking a banana. The banana was just a regular old fruit, not a super-powered piece of food like the Magic Pickle or the bad egg. The banana was supposed to be the gibbon's afternoon treat, but now it was just a soggy mess.

The Magic Pickle listened as the egg shook the banana in his gooey, drippy hands.

"Won't talk, eh?" snarled the Egg Poacher. "What, you think this is gonna be *over easy*? I know he's here somewhere! You better tell me! They don't call me the Egg Poacher for nuthin'!"

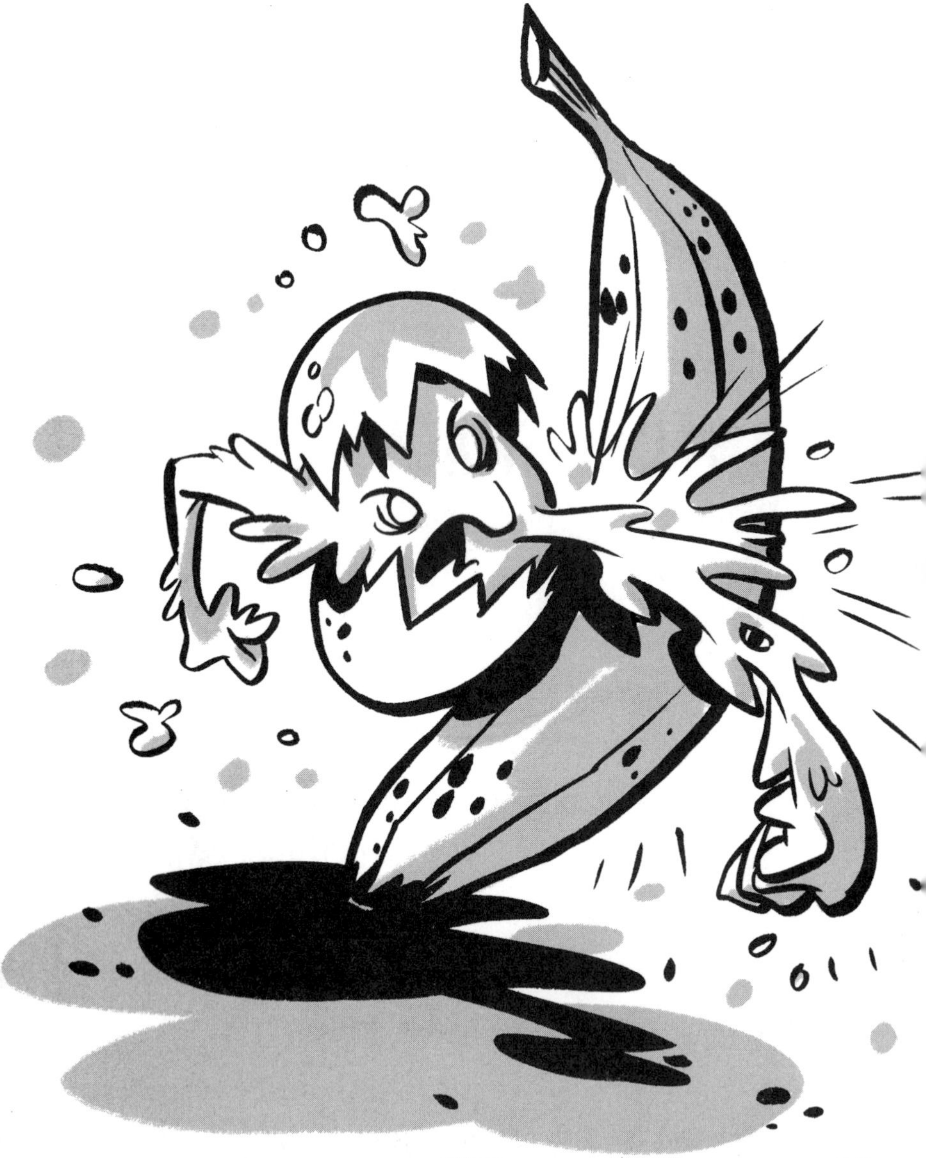

The Magic Pickle leaned in.

"The Brotherhood sent me and I'll find him!" the bad egg continued, unaware that he was being watched. "They said they'd pay a bundle if I found him and got him to join up! They're lookin' for the wildest fruit in town, and I'll find him!"

The Egg Poacher threw the banana to the ground. It squirted out of the peel. A chattering gibbon monkey swung down and grabbed it.

CHITCHITCHIT!
HOOW HOOW HOOW!

"Awww, look on the sunny side," the egg said to the gibbon. "I squashed it up for you. Now you don't gotta chew it!"

SMACK!

A green, briny fist connected with hard shell. The evil egg spun around and fell against the nearby monkey bars. The Magic Pickle hovered over him.

"Speaking of squash," he said, "it looks like you may end up an omelet unless you crack and tell me why you're tearing the zoo apart!"

"With lines like that, yer really *crack-in'* me up!" the Egg Poacher replied. He rubbed the new crack on his shelly head. "You wanna hear a *yolk*? What did the free-range hen send the slimy old cucumber for his birthday?"

The Magic Pickle stopped to think.

"An eggbeater!" shouted the bad egg. A long, stringy, slimy arm shot out of the cracked eggshell and nailed the Magic Pickle on the head.

SMACK!

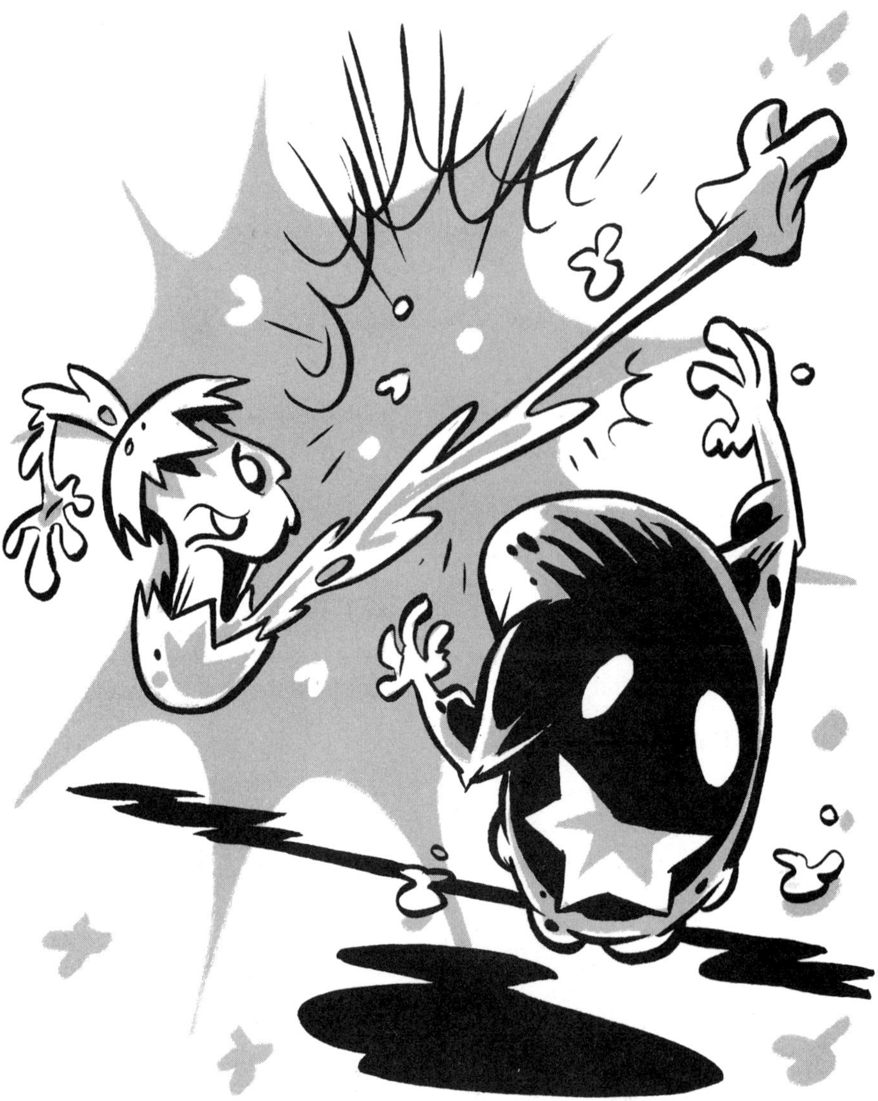

The Magic Pickle toppled over and landed in a bowl full of bananas.

"I gotta make my eggs-it," laughed the bad egg. "See ya!"

The bad egg rolled away and disappeared into the zoo.

A gibbon swung down and plucked the Magic Pickle from the bowl of bananas. The little ape pulled a soggy banana peel off the Magic Pickle's head and quickly opened his mouth wide, ready to take a bite.

"Don't even *think* about it," the Magic Pickle ordered.

WWAAAHHHGGG!!!

The gibbon screamed and dropped the talking dill. The monkey scrambled up to a high branch and hid.

"I've got to put an end to that oval offender," said the Magic Pickle. He zoomed off into the zoo, hot on the trail of the Egg Poacher.

Chapter 7

"**H**old on, Ellen!" shouted Jo Jo. "I'll get you down; just don't move around or you might fall!"

Jo Jo climbed to the roof of the Reptile House to help Ellen find a way down safely. When she made it to the top, she saw there was egg goop everywhere!

"*What* . . . ???" Jo Jo gasped. "ELLEN!

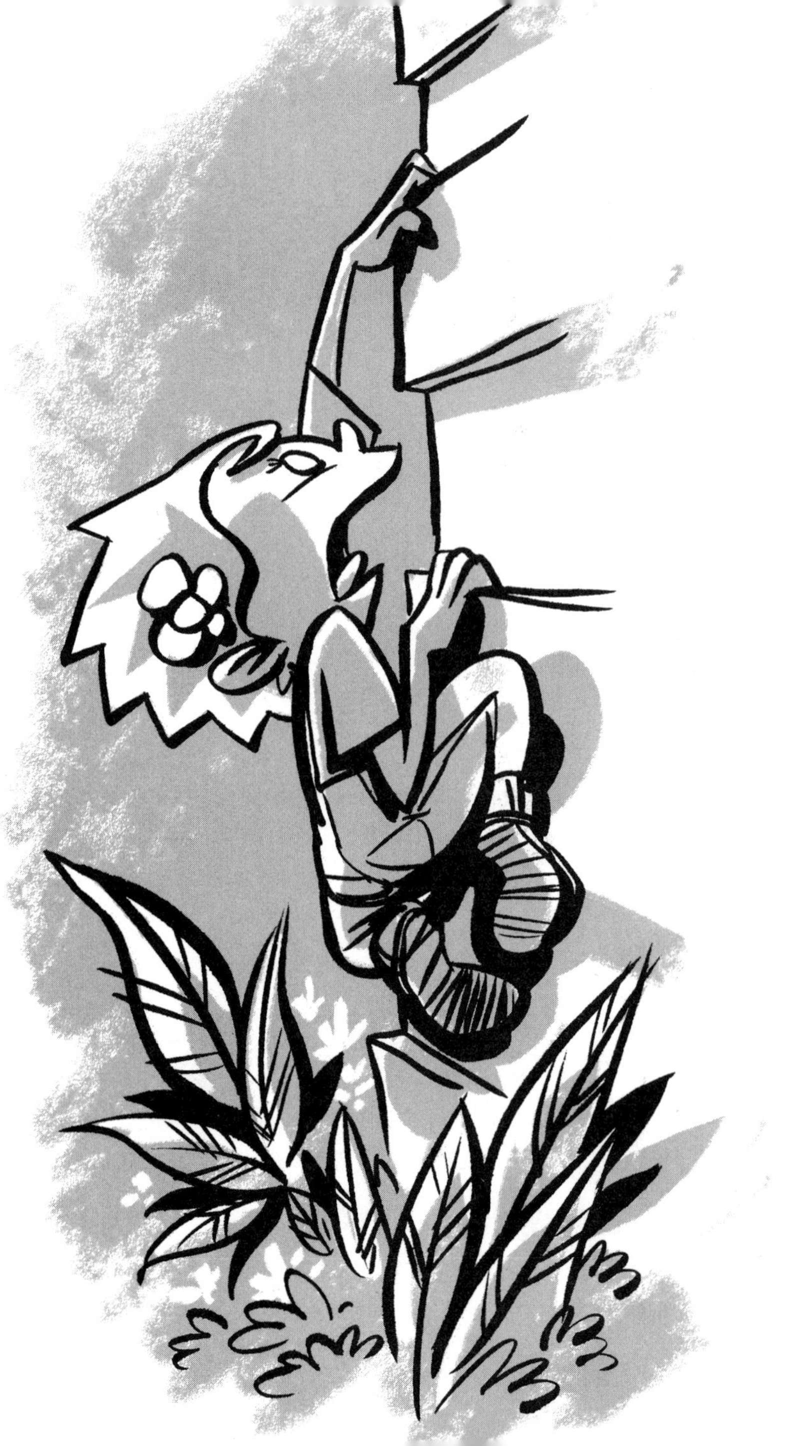

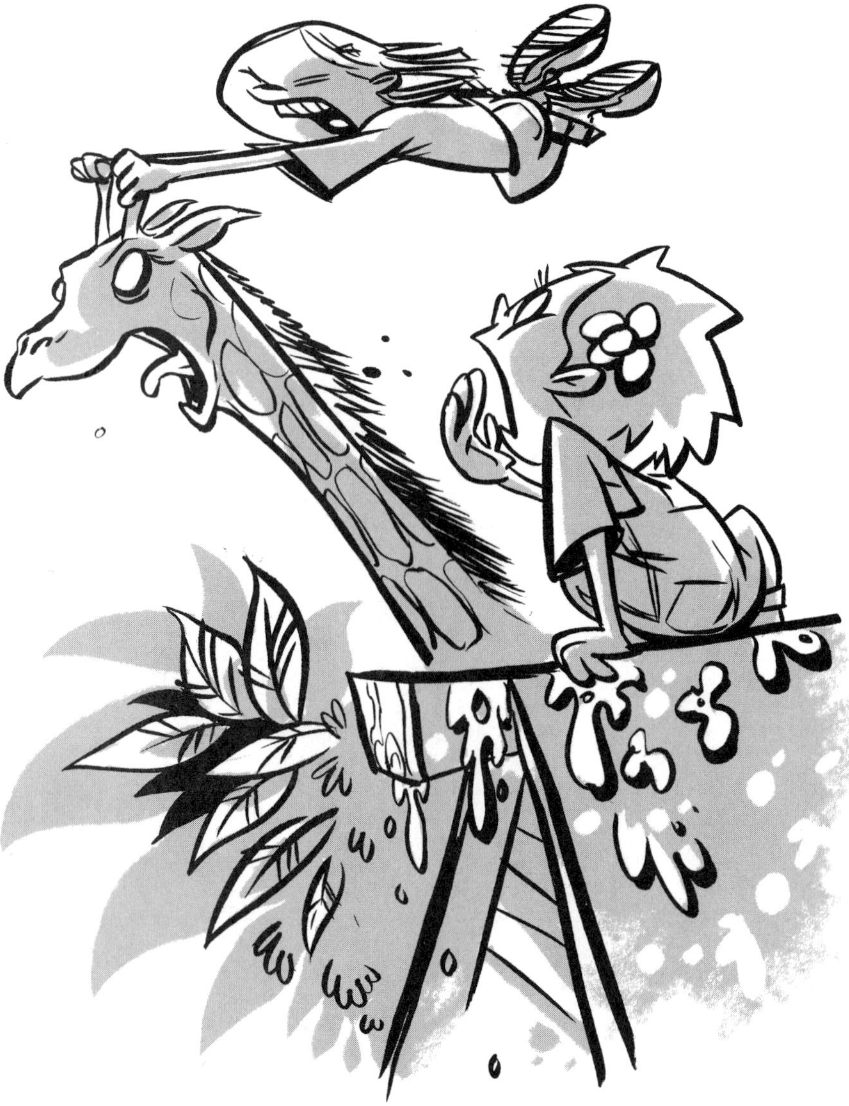

Where did you go?!"

"I'm over **HEEEERRRRREEE!!!**" Ellen squealed.

Jo Jo's jaw dropped. Ellen was holding on tight to a giraffe's small horns.

"How the heck did you get up there?" asked Jo Jo. "Or should I ask, how the *neck* did you get up there?!"

"I don't know!" squeaked Ellen. "One second I'm sitting on the Reptile House, the next second, I'm sliding down this guy's neck!"

"Well, stay still!" Jo Jo called. She spied an overhanging tree branch and jumped.

Ellen's giraffe saw the leaves rustle on the end of Jo Jo's branch. The giraffe licked its lips with a hungry look and walked toward Jo Jo's tree.

"All right, here he comes. Just jump when I count three!" Jo Jo yelled to Ellen.

"One!

"Two!"

The giraffe stepped closer and swung its head toward Jo Jo.

"THREE! Jump!" Jo Jo yelled.

"AAAIIEEE!!!" screamed Ellen.

POOSH!!!

Ellen landed in a big ostrich nest. The mother ostrich reached in and nuzzled Ellen's face.

"Oh, man." Jo Jo squinted.

"Um . . . help . . . ?" Ellen giggled as the mother ostrich pecked gently at her long hair.

"I'll go for help!" Jo Jo said. "Stay put and don't let them nest in your hair."

Chapter 8

"**H**ey, vinegar head!" Jo Jo yelled.

The Magic Pickle was zooming by. He stopped midair and hovered over to where Jo Jo sat on her tree branch above Ellen.

"I see you're monkeying around while I'm out trying to beat the Egg Poacher," said the Magic Pickle.

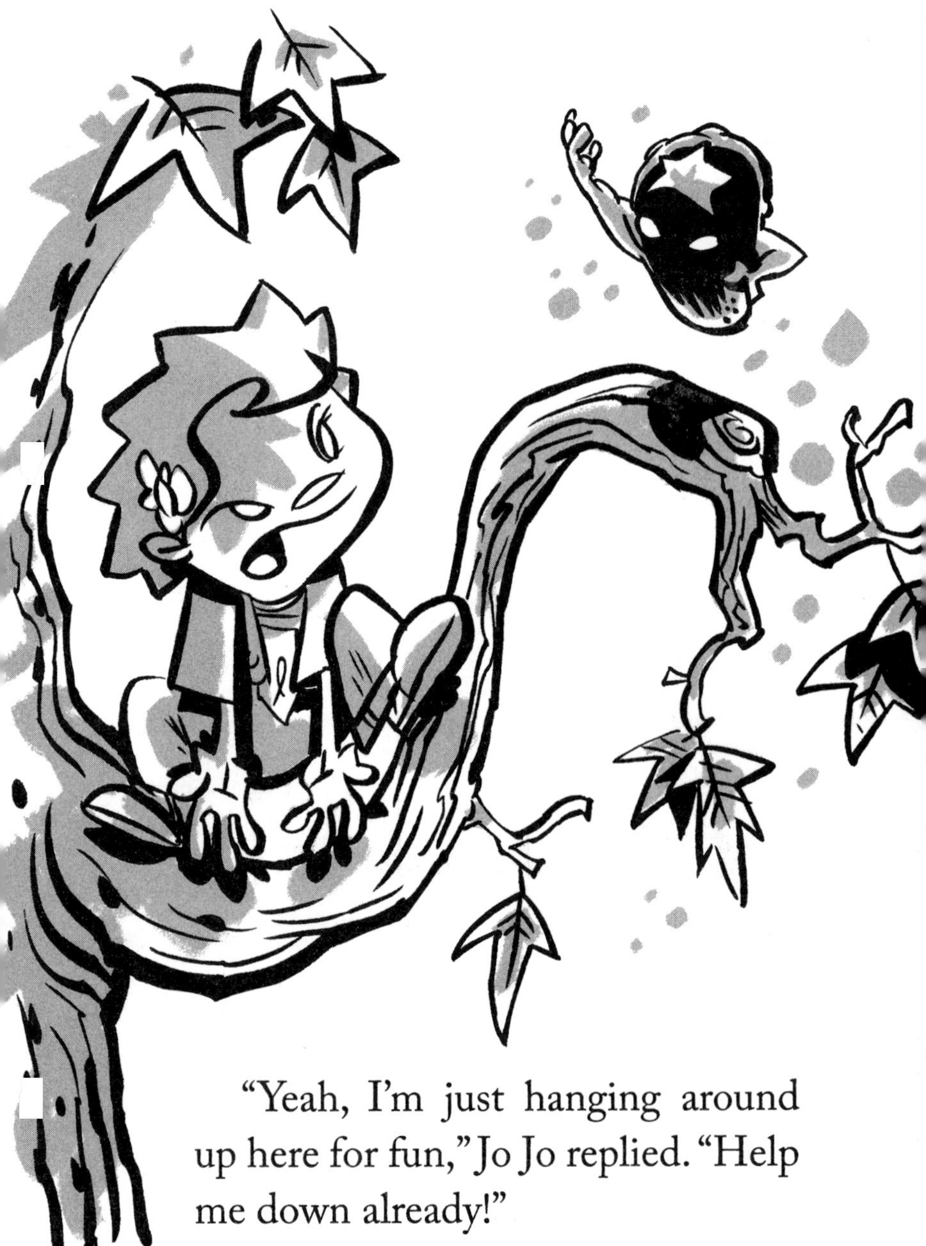

"Yeah, I'm just hanging around up here for fun," Jo Jo replied. "Help me down already!"

The Magic Pickle lowered Jo Jo safely to the ground.

"I encountered our round renegade in the gibbon habitat," the Magic Pickle said. "It appears he's left the zookeepers quite a mess to deal with."

Jo Jo turned around and spotted four

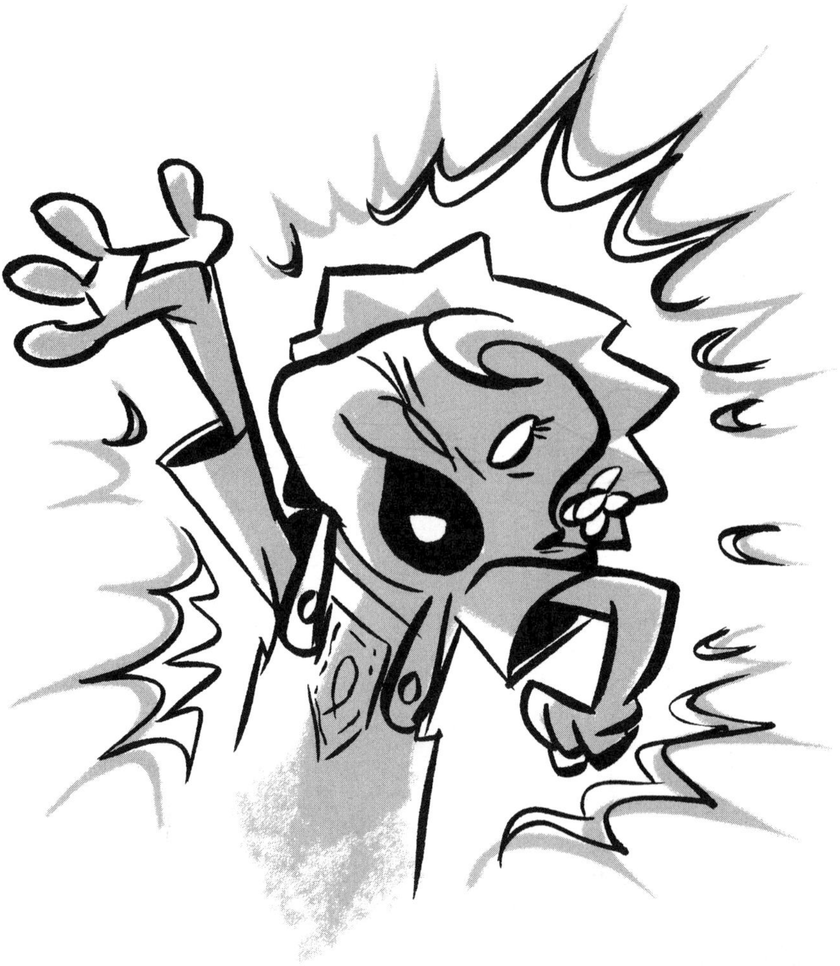

zookeepers running frantically after a small herd of zebras. Two more keepers were trying to coax a bear out of a tree. The zoo was a complete mess. Animals ran rampant. Gooey egg slime dripped here and there, evidence of the Egg Poacher's trail.

"I overheard that hard-shelled criminal say he was here on behalf of the Brotherhood of Evil Produce," the Magic Pickle continued. "He's apparently trying to recruit someone from the zoo to join the Brotherhood."

"Well, that can't be good," said Jo Jo. "Who does he mean?"

"Indeed not," agreed the Magic Pickle. "The bad egg said he was looking for the 'wildest' fruit in town."

"Well, everything here is 'wild,' you know?" Jo Jo said. "It's a zoo!"

"We've got to crack this," the Magic Pickle said urgently. "Think! What could he be after?!"

"This is driving me batty!" said Jo Jo. "What animal has anything to do with food?"

"Jo Jo! You're a genius!" cried the Magic Pickle. He grabbed her arm and pulled her along.

"What?! Where are we going?!" she cried.

"The Rodent House!" said the Magic Pickle.

Chapter 9

BAAASSSHHH!!!

The doors to the Rodent House crashed open and smashed to bits. Rats, mice, and gophers peered anxiously from their glass habitats.

The Egg Poacher oozed into the room. Egg white dripped from his cracked shell and splattered in droplets to the ground.

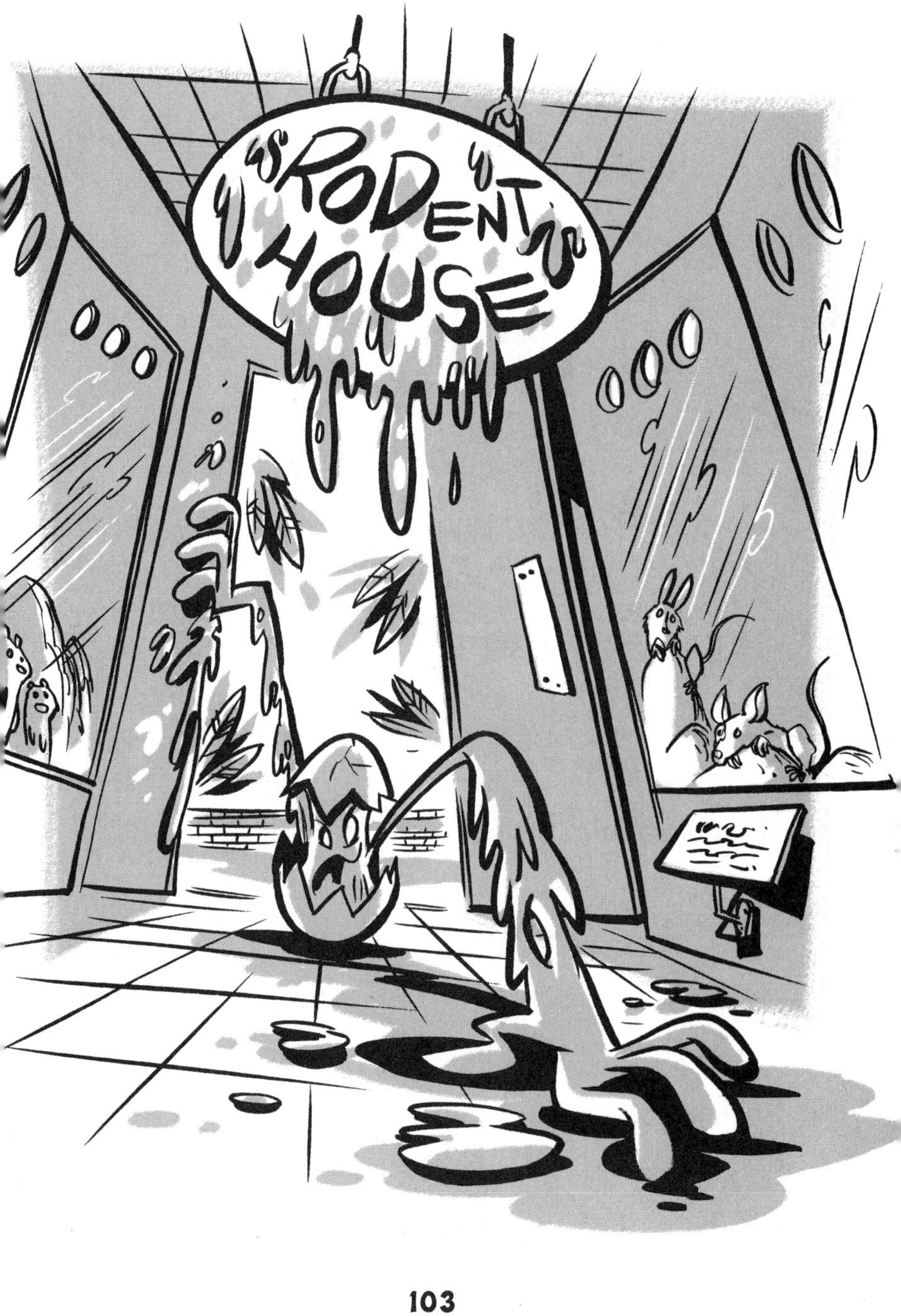
RODENT HOUSE

The evil egg stopped, his eyes wide. He grinned a yolky grin.

He stared at one glass habitat in particular. The sign below it read:

FRUIT BAT

"Now we're gettin' somewhere," said the Egg Poacher. "I'm lookin' for someone, and you just might know where I can find him!"

A small bat hung silently upside down in its habitat.

"I've been sent by the Brotherhood of Evil Produce," said the bad egg. "You ever heard of the Brotherhood?"

The fruit bat yawned.

"Don't get all hard-boiled on *me*!" shouted the Egg Poacher. "The Brotherhood is the rottenest bunch of table scraps in town, and they'll let me join up if I can convince the Wild Kiwi to join up, too! So where is he?!"

The fruit bat blinked.

"See, I'm just an egg, not a fruit or veggie. The Brotherhood only lets fruits and veggies become full members," said the Egg Poacher, "unless I can convince this Wild Kiwi guy to join up, too. So spill! Where's the fruit, fruit bat?"

The bad egg thrust a gooey, stringy egg-white hand through a small airhole and grabbed the fruit bat.

SQUELCH!

He pulled the fruit bat toward the glass.

"They say the Wild Kiwi turned loose a horde of fruit flies on Australia. He single-handedly held a crate of apples ransom until their due dates expired. He's *wild*, man. And the Brotherhood wants him on their side to help wipe out the Magic Pickle and bring on the fabled Salad Days, when they'll rule the world!"

The Egg Poacher looked the fruit bat in the eye.

"Now, where can I find this Wild Kiwi?" he demanded.

"Unhand that winged mouse, you cartonless criminal!" shouted the Magic Pickle.

BOOOSSHHH!

A blast of vinegar-enhanced energy smushed the egg against the glass wall. The evil egg dropped the fruit bat. The bat flew up to an eave, hung upside down, and licked egg slime from his wings.

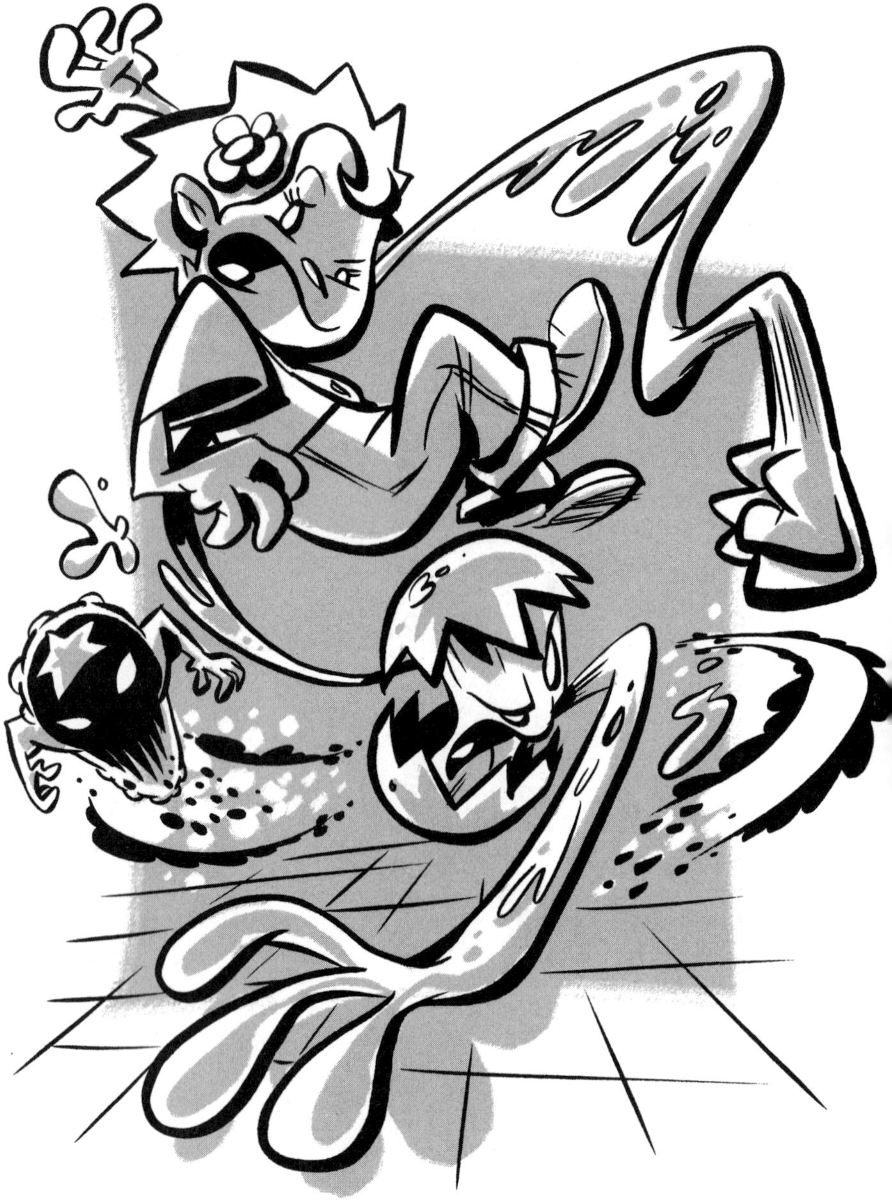

"You ain't gonna stop me, pickle-breath!" shouted the Egg Poacher. "I'm gonna find that Wild Kiwi, and when I do, we're gonna join the Brotherhood and turn you into a sliced-up burger topping!"

"I'll relish watching you fry," said the Magic Pickle.

"You want to kidnap a *kiwi*?!" asked Jo Jo.

"I'll kidnap him if he won't join up, poach him if I have to!" laughed the bad egg. "Either way, I'm gettin' into the ranks of the Brotherhood, and you ain't gonna stand in my way!"

The Egg Poacher rolled away fast. He tumbled right past the Magic Pickle and Jo Jo and out the door of the Rodent House.

Chapter 10

Jo Jo ran along as the Magic Pickle flew overhead. They searched the zoo grounds for any sign of the Egg Poacher. The zookeepers had managed to herd in some of the elephants, but the gorillas had hijacked a security cart and were taking it for a joyride.

"Where do you think he'll strike next?" asked Jo Jo.

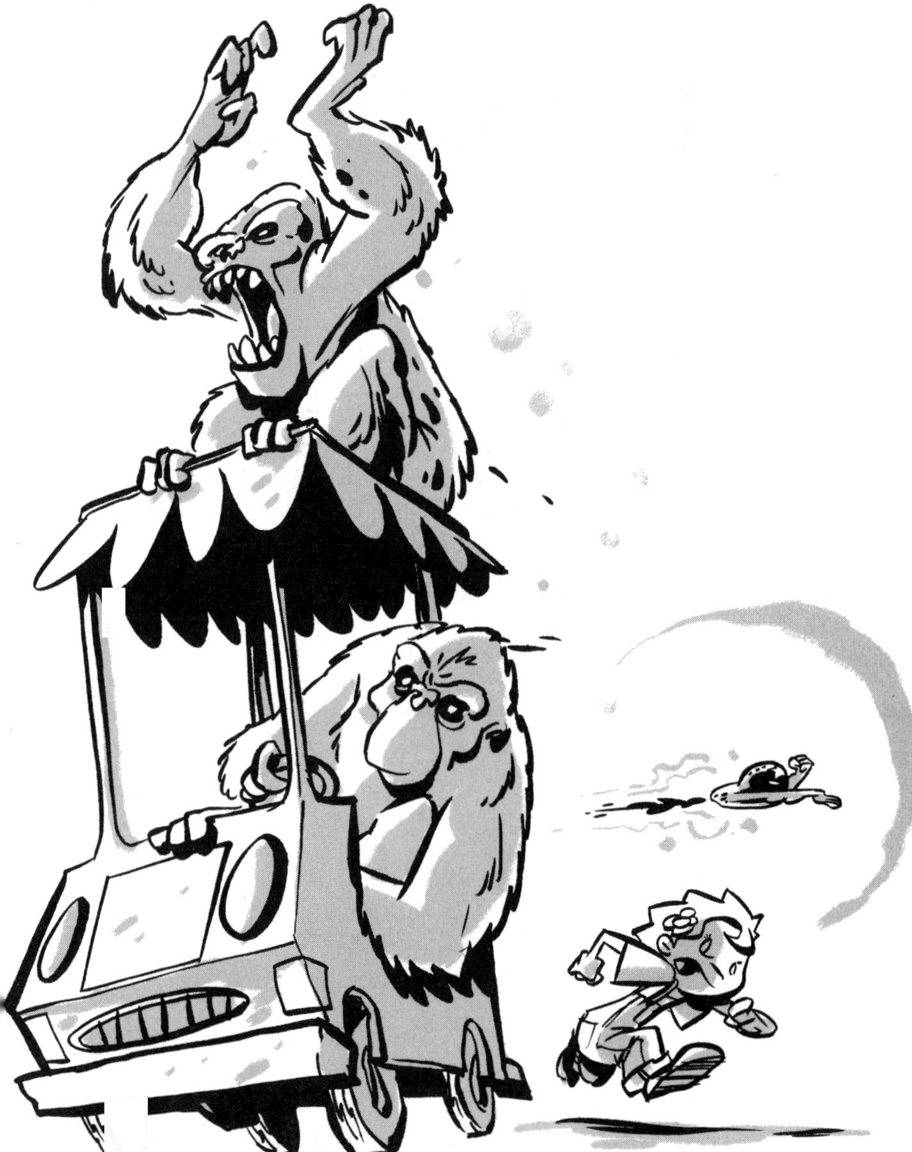

"That egg is scrambled," the Magic Pickle said. "He seems to think that the fruit bat could help him find this mysterious 'Wild Kiwi' character. I think he might be mixed up."

"Of course!" realized Jo Jo. "I bet he thought the fruit bat was really a fruit! And you know, now that I think of it, I just realized something else!"

"Speak, girl," the Magic Pickle urged. "The fate of the world may be at hand."

"A kiwi is indeed a fruit," Jo Jo said, "but it's also a type of bird, with a really long beak, from New Zealand!"

Jo Jo grabbed the Magic Pickle by the hand and dragged him into the exotic-bird aviary. They looked around frantically.

"See? Over there!" Jo Jo pointed. "*The Wild Kiwi!*"

Jo Jo and the Magic Pickle stared at a habitat filled with three or four wild kiwi

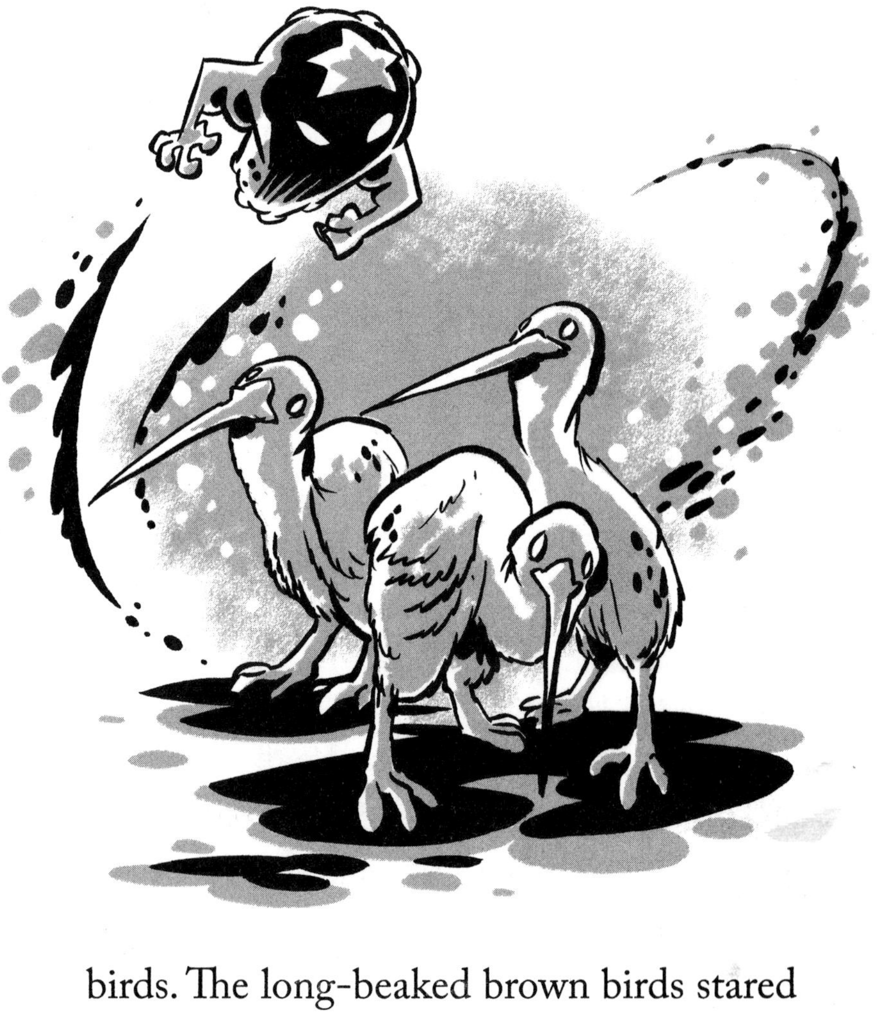

birds. The long-beaked brown birds stared back.

"Well, I'll be salted and buttered," exclaimed the Magic Pickle. "They're a strange-looking specimen of bird, all right."

"I bet there isn't even a real 'Wild Kiwi' bad guy," said Jo Jo. "I bet it's all just made up, like some sort of test to see if the Egg Poacher is smart enough to join the Brotherhood!"

"Well, we've clearly seen his brains are a bit fried," said the Magic Pickle. "Not your typical egghead."

The wild kiwi birds fluttered a bit and pecked at some seeds on the floor. Jo Jo read aloud from the display information.

"The sign here says kiwis can't fly," said Jo Jo.

"A pity. I highly recommend flight as an economic mode of travel," the Magic Pickle told the birds.

A kiwi sat snuggled atop a small egg.

"Bravo, that's the right idea," chuckled the Magic Pickle. "Hold that egg down

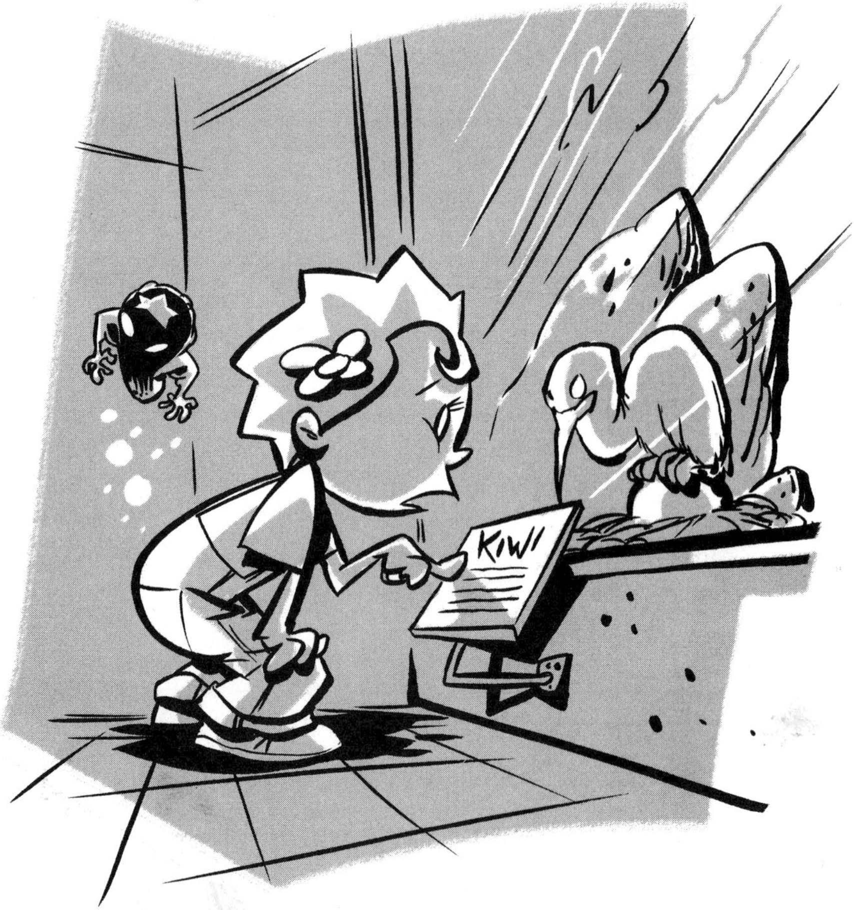
KIWI

until the authorities arrive!"

"That's her baby, ya green goof," said Jo Jo.

"I'm aware of that fact," the Magic Pickle said quickly. "I was making a yolk."

“A bad yolk,” sighed Jo Jo. She pulled out her pad of paper and wrote down some notes about the wild kiwi birds.

“All right, at least we’ve got our facts straight now,” Jo Jo said once she finished.

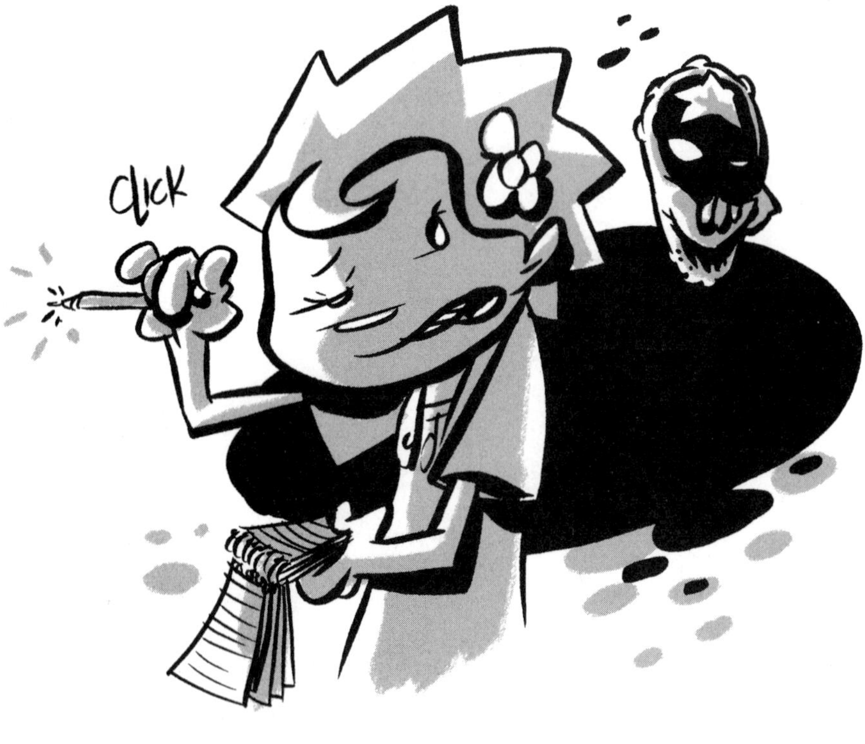
CLICK

Chapter 11

Jo Jo and the Magic Pickle stepped out of the aviary and into the sunlight. The zookeepers had regained control of their security cart and had the gorillas safely in the backseat. But now a flock of penguins had joined forces with a polar bear and raided the snack bar. Popcorn spilled onto the sidewalk. A turtle slowly walked off

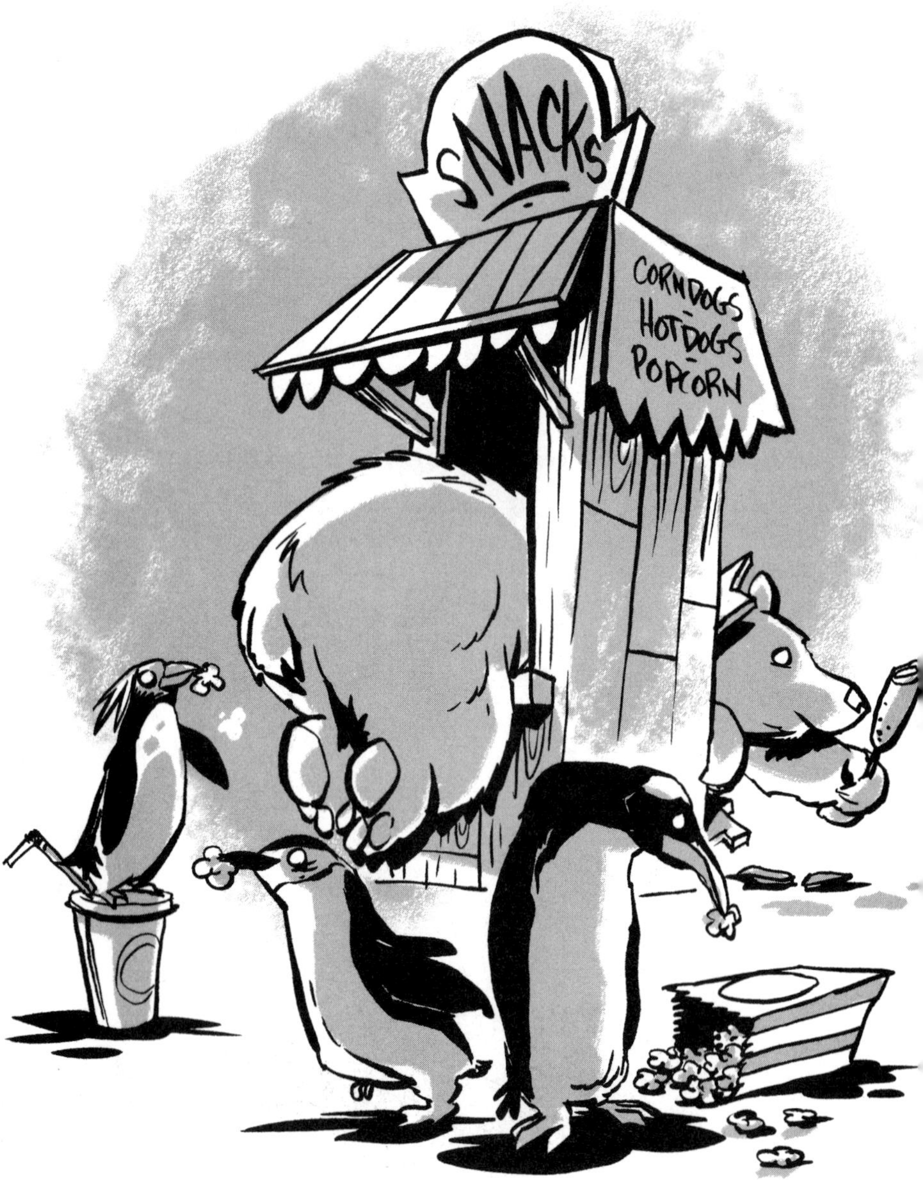
SNACKS
CORNDOGS
HOTDOGS
POPCORN

with a giant-size paper cup on its back. A small rabbit sat inside, sipping soda and hitching a ride.

Over at the zoo entrance, a tiger sat on the chair inside the ticket booth.

"How much if you're over sixty-five years of age?" asked a little old lady at the ticket booth. She squinted into her purse. "I get a senior-citizen discount!"

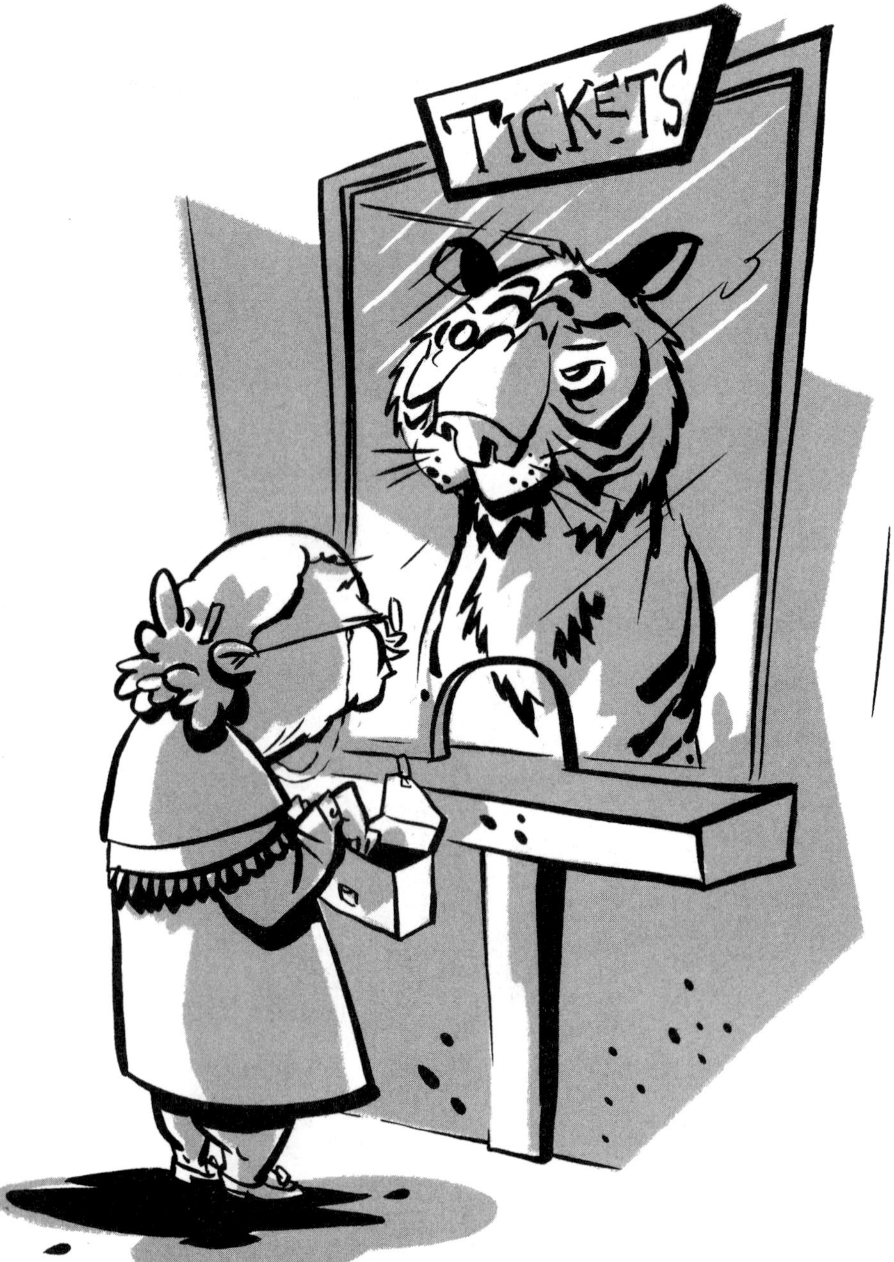
TICKETS

RRROOOWWWWRRRR!!!!

The tiger bristled its whiskers at her.

"Well, you don't have to be rude," the old lady snapped. She turned away and waddled off.

HYEEEAHYEAHHYEAHHH!

A pack of hyenas sat nearby and cackled.

"Hey look! An egg!" Jo Jo yelled and pointed.

"Get him!" cried the Magic Pickle.

Sure enough, an egg was rolling down the path ahead. Jo Jo and the Magic Pickle gave chase.

"He's going into the Reptile House!" said Jo Jo. "I was in there earlier with . . ."

"Well, you'll know your way around, then," said the Magic Pickle.

GASP!!!

". . . *with Ellen!!*" cried Jo Jo. "Oh, no! I was supposed to get help. I hope Ellen's doing OK!"

"Onward!" said the Magic Pickle and they went into the Reptile House.

Girl and pickle rounded a corner and stared down the hall of habitats.

"There he is! EGG! Get him!" shouted Jo Jo.

The cracked egg rolled to a stop. Jo Jo ran forward.

"Wait!" ordered the Magic Pickle.

"That's not our evil egg. It appears to be a turtle egg."

"What?! How do you know?" asked Jo Jo, ready to pounce.

"Because there's a turtle coming out of

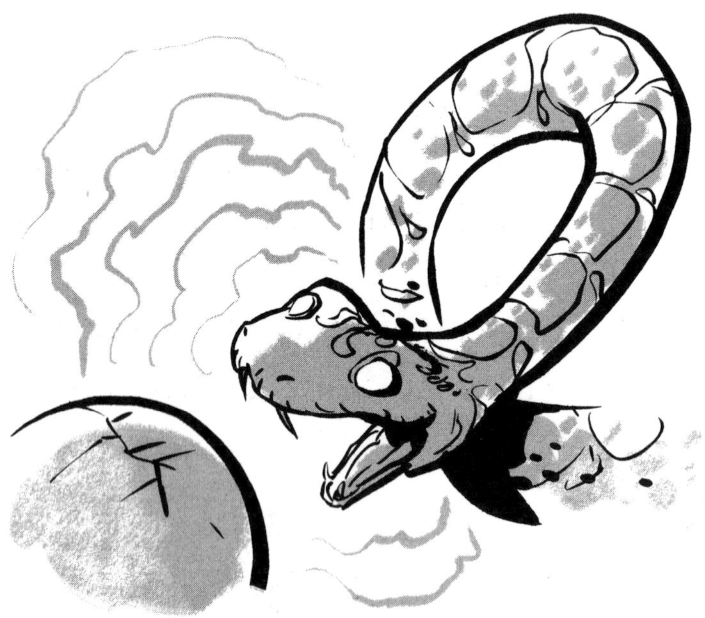

it," the Magic Pickle said matter-of-factly.

The egg shook a bit, then cracked open all the way. A baby turtle opened its eyes, looking up at them.

HHHIIIssssssssss!

Suddenly, a quick slithering movement caught their attention. Something was lunging for the egg.

"Not on my watch, serpent!" shouted the Magic Pickle.

In a flash of green, the dill hero pinched the snake behind the head and lifted it into the air, harmless.

"Hey! That snake is an egg eater!" Jo Jo said. She flipped through her notes. "A *Dasypeltis scabra*!"

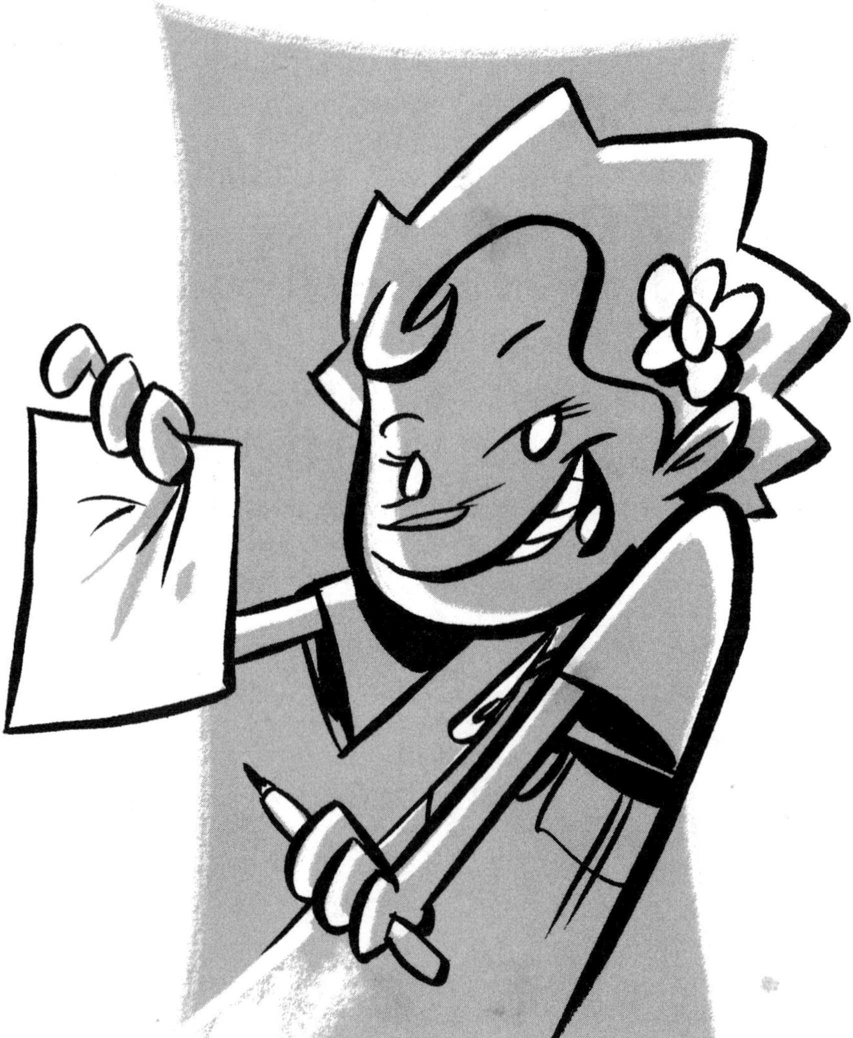

"He'll have no meal while I'm around," said the Magic Pickle. The baby turtle blinked at him.

"Wait, maybe he *should*!" said Jo Jo excitedly.

"Explain yourself," the Magic Pickle demanded.

"I've got an idea!" said Jo Jo with a smile. She pulled some paper from her notepad and began to draw. "You find a holding pen for that snake. I've got some signs to make!"

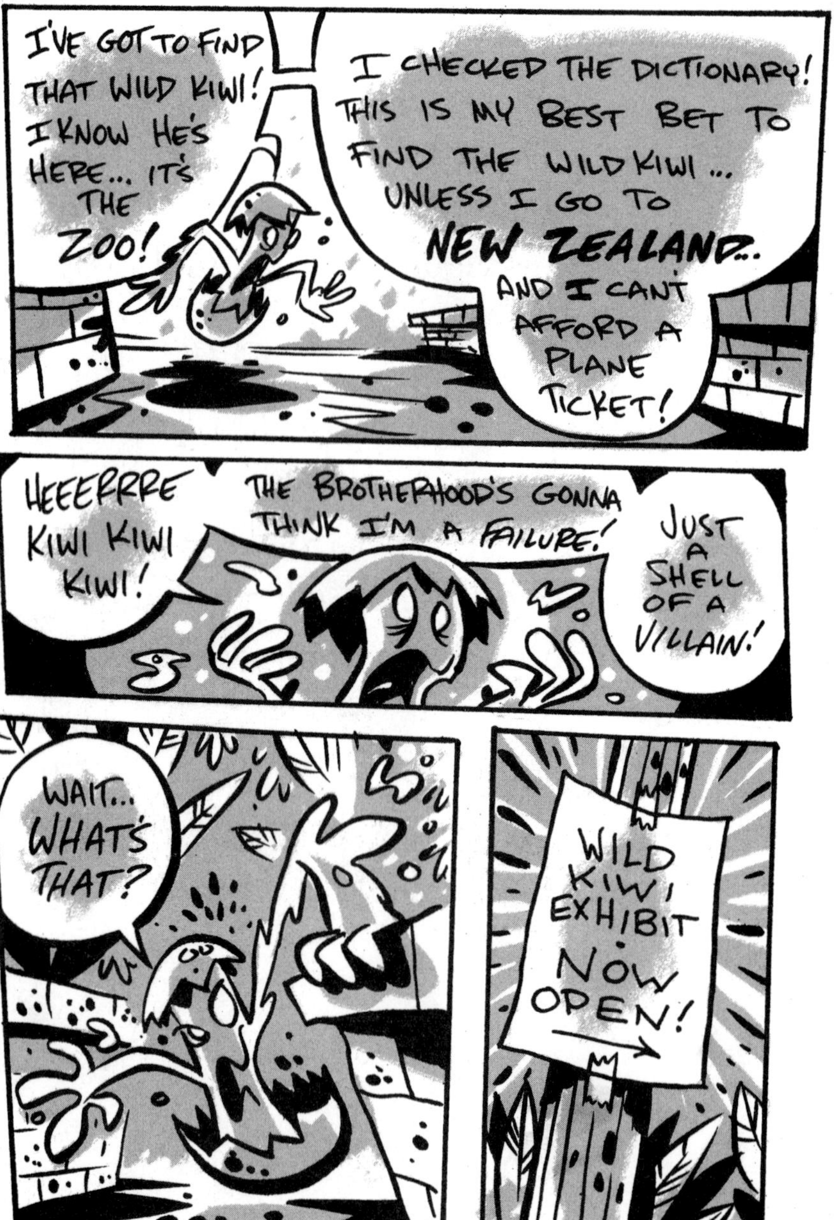
I'VE GOT TO FIND THAT WILD KIWI! I KNOW HE'S HERE... IT'S THE ZOO!
I CHECKED THE DICTIONARY! THIS IS MY BEST BET TO FIND THE WILD KIWI... UNLESS I GO TO NEW ZEALAND...
AND I CAN'T AFFORD A PLANE TICKET!
HEEERRRE KIWI KIWI KIWI!
THE BROTHERHOOD'S GONNA THINK I'M A FAILURE!
JUST A SHELL OF A VILLAIN!
WAIT... WHAT'S THAT?
WILD KIWI EXHIBIT NOW OPEN!

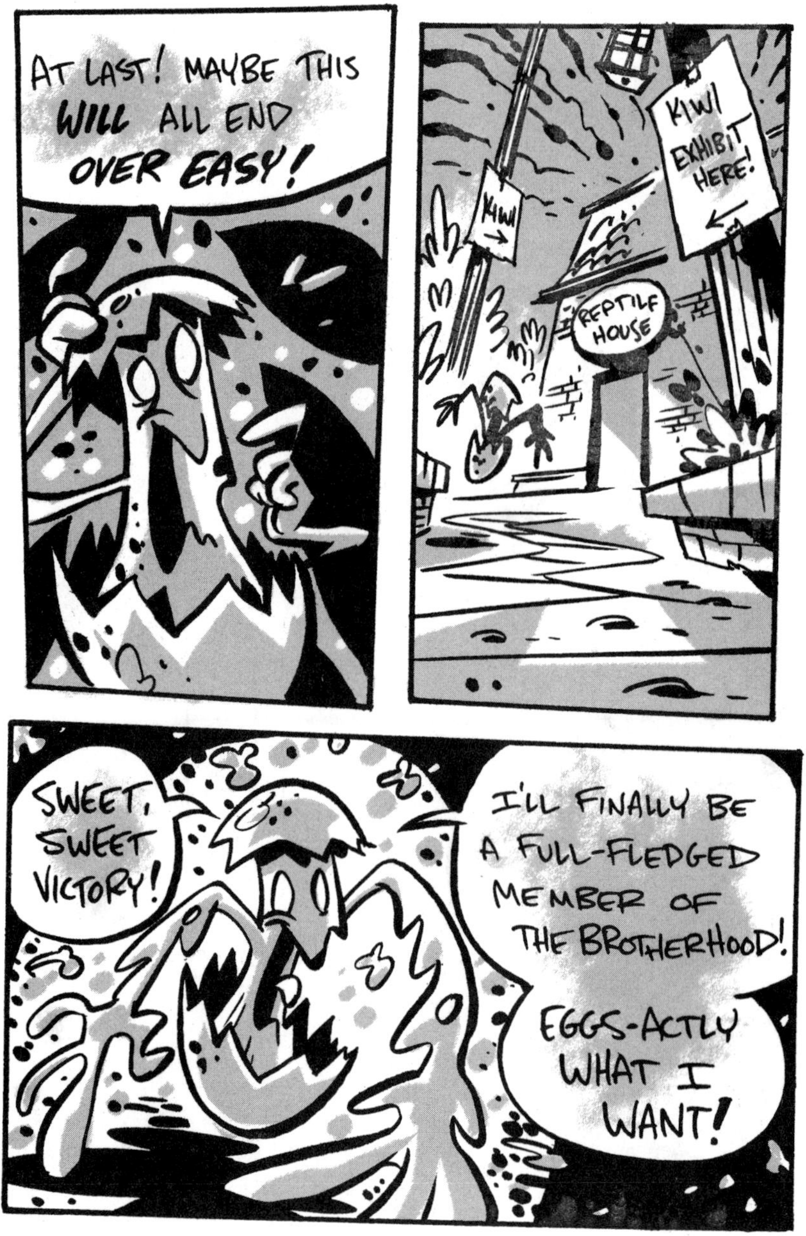
AT LAST! MAYBE THIS WILL ALL END OVER EASY!
KIWI EXHIBIT HERE!
KIWI
REPTILE HOUSE
SWEET, SWEET VICTORY!
I'LL FINALLY BE A FULL-FLEDGED MEMBER OF THE BROTHERHOOD!
EGGS-ACTLY WHAT I WANT!

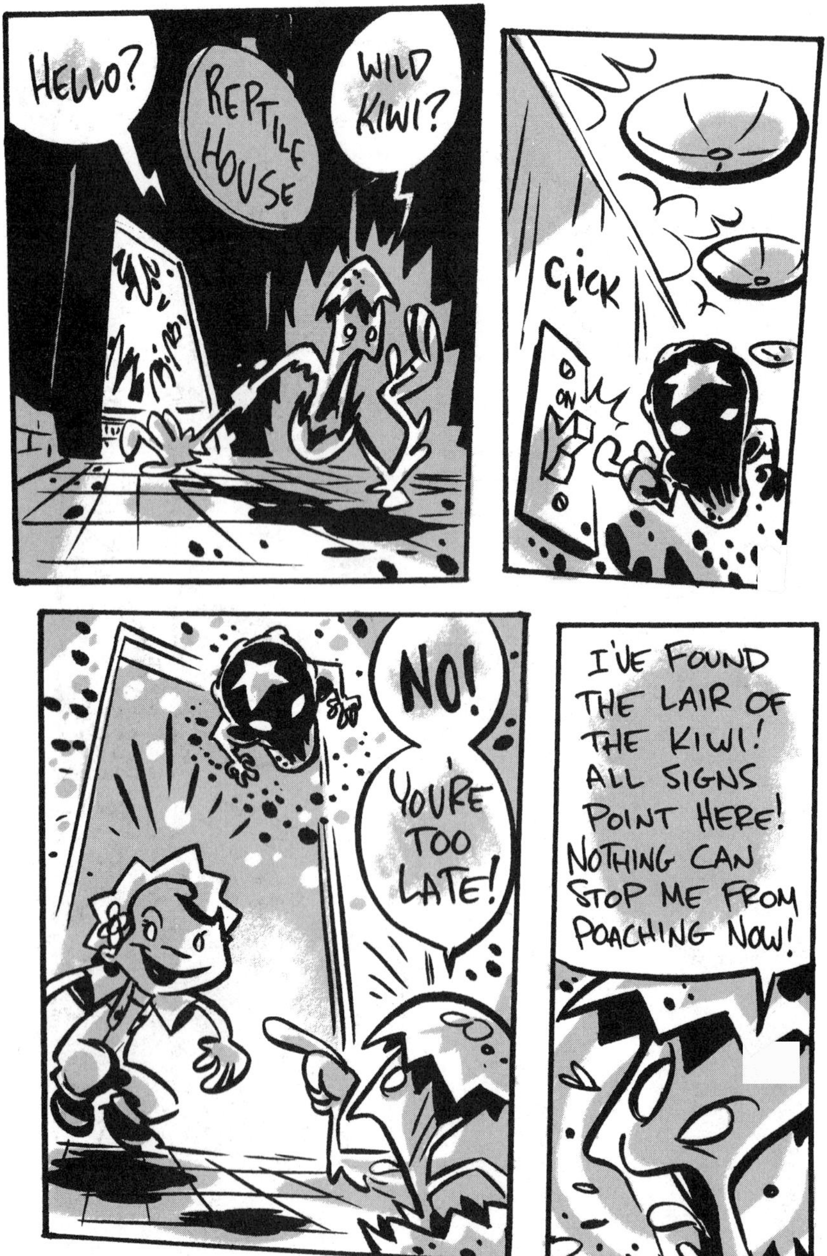
HELLO?
REPTILE HOUSE
WILD KIWI?
CLICK
ON
NO!
YOU'RE TOO LATE!
I'VE FOUND THE LAIR OF THE KIWI! ALL SIGNS POINT HERE! NOTHING CAN STOP ME FROM POACHING NOW!

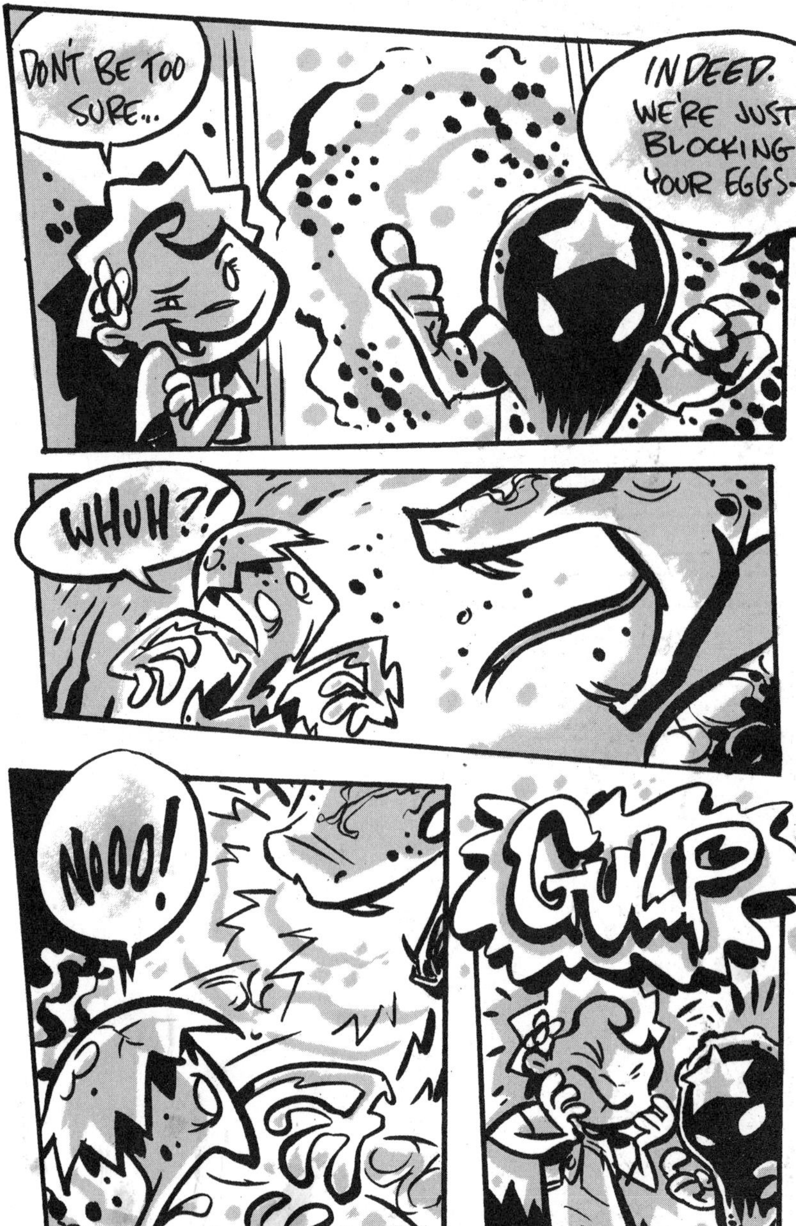
DON'T BE TOO SURE...
INDEED. WE'RE JUST BLOCKING YOUR EGGS-IT!
WHUH?!
NOOO!
GULP

Chapter 12

By late afternoon, the zoo was almost completely back to normal. All of the drippy, gooey egg whites had been mopped up. The animals had all returned to their habitats and were resting in the shade.

When Miss Emilyek and the class assembled at the zoo's entrance, Jo Jo and Ellen slipped into the back of the group

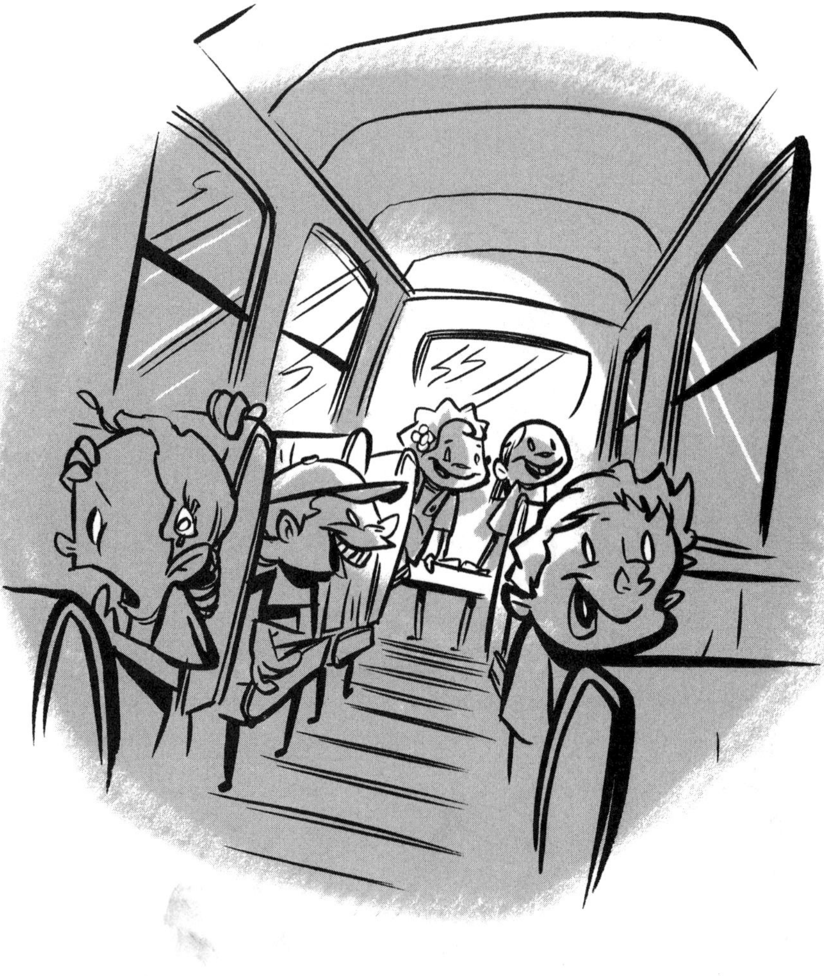

of students. Luckily, in all the mayhem, no one had noticed they were gone.

"Did you see the kangaroos jumping over the gator pit?" one kid asked.

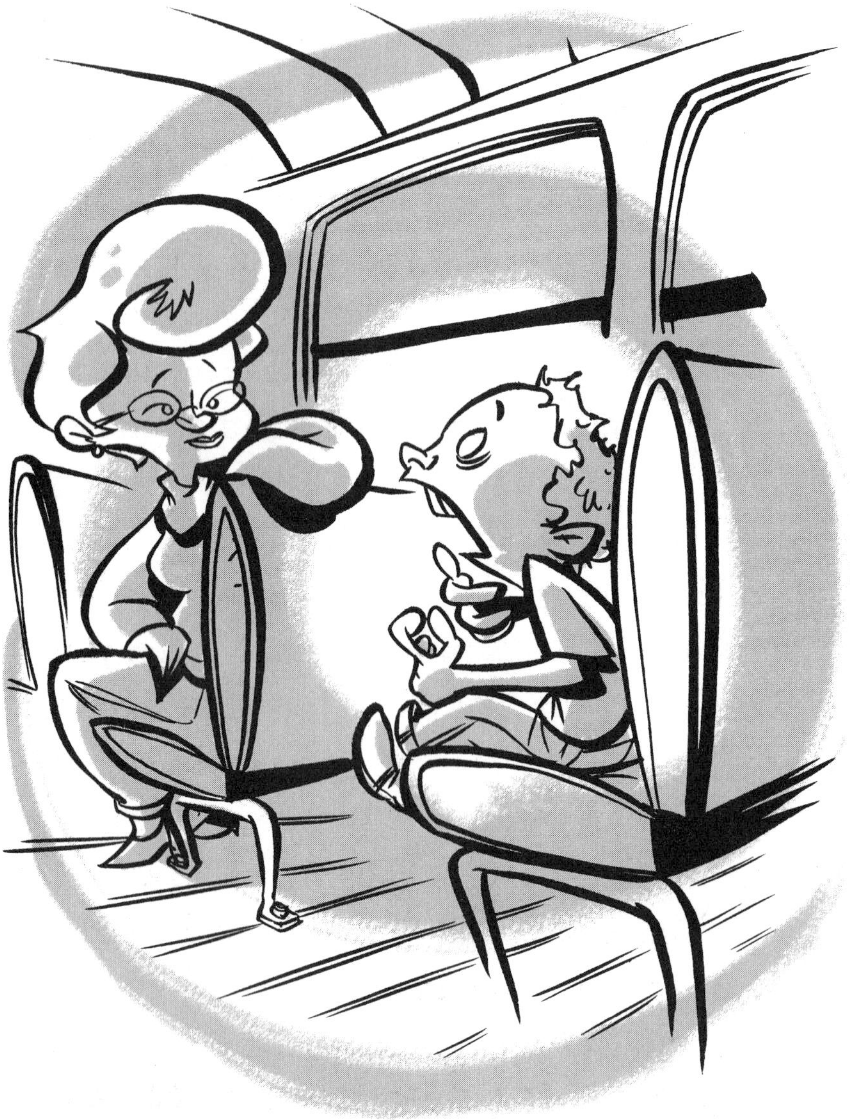

"I missed that," answered another kid. "I got knocked over by an armadillo. They were playing bowling with the chimps."

"There's a seat for two," said Jo Jo. She grabbed Ellen's hand and the girls sat down. Jo Jo stowed her backpack under her seat, but not before the Magic Pickle gave her a quick wink from inside it. Ellen tried to fix her hair, but the ostriches had given her a whole new look.

"Uggg, my hair looks like a bird's nest," Ellen moaned.

"You'll be OK in the morning, after you wash it," assured Jo Jo. "At least that ostrich didn't try to adopt you! It's a good thing I showed up and traded you for a bunch of lettuce from the snack bar sandwiches."

"You're tellin' me!" agreed Ellen. "I'd have to learn to sleep with my head buried in the sand."

VRRRVRRRROOOOMMMM!

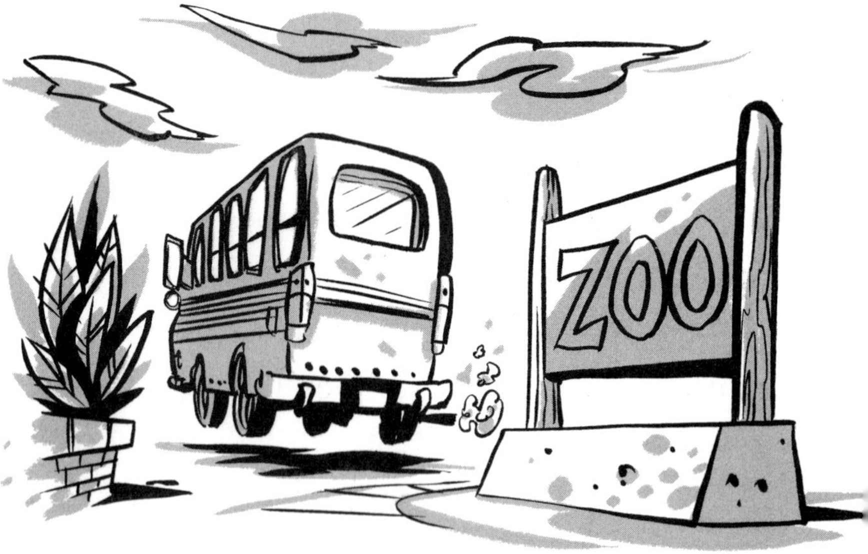
ZOO

The school bus rumbled down the road. They were on their way.

"Class, let's see what we all learned today," announced Miss Emilyek from the front of the bus. "Did any pair of 'buddies' manage to gather five fun facts?"

"Miss Emilyek," said Mikey, "I don't know how anyone could have gathered *any* facts with all those wild animals on the loose! I mean, did you *see* those gorillas? They drive a cart better than my dad does on the golf course. I was FREAKED OUT!"

The other kids loudly agreed.

"Wait, Miss Emilyek." Jo Jo's hand shot up. "Ellen and I have five fun facts!"

"We do?!" asked Ellen, surprised. "Is one of them that I got clobbered by a flying monkey?"

"Go ahead, Jo Jo!" said Miss Emilyek.

Jo Jo pulled out her pad of paper and began to read her notes. "One: We found out that there's a big lizard called a goanna, whose name is pronounced with a hard G sound."

Ellen joined in. "Two: We learned that boa constrictors are smooth!"

"Three," continued Jo Jo, "we learned that kiwis are not only fruits, they're also birds, from New Zealand, and they can't fly."

"We learned that?" Ellen asked under her breath.

"I took some notes while you were busy with the ostriches," said Jo Jo.

"Oh," said Ellen, patting her hair. "Cool."

"Oh, yeah!" said Ellen. "Number four: I guess I learned that giraffes like to eat leaves! The one I was riding went straight for a bunch of them right before I got accidentally smacked off!"

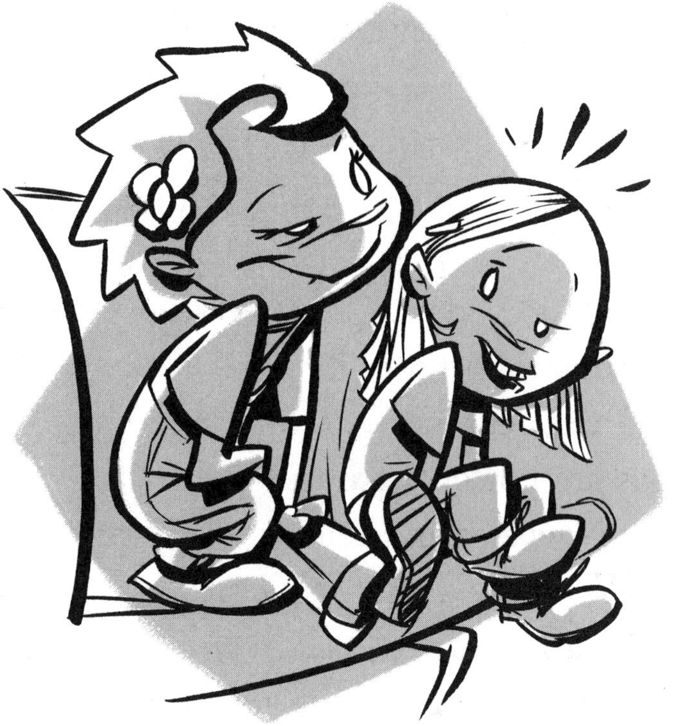

HAHAHAHAHAHA!

Jo Jo's backpack shook a bit near her feet. Jo Jo leaned down and peeked in.

"Pssst. Don't forget the hero of the day," the Magic Pickle whispered through the flap of the backpack. "I mean, besides us, of course."

"And five!" said Jo Jo, "there's a type of snake from Africa called the *Dasypeltis scabra*!"

"And can you tell us something special about that snake, Jo Jo?" asked Miss Emilyek.

"Yep!" Jo Jo grinned. "It eats eggs!"

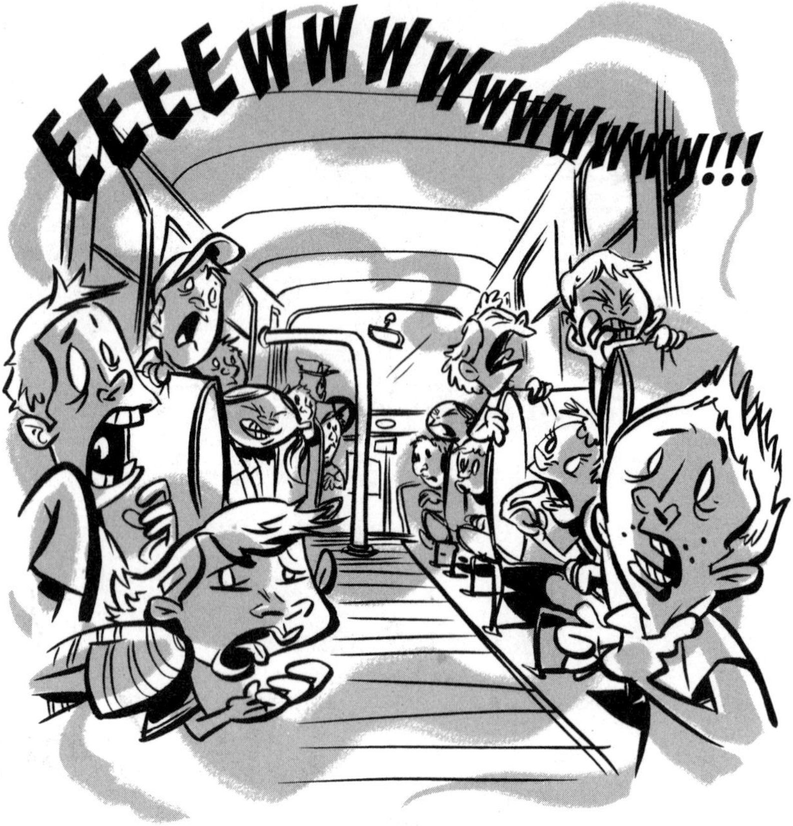
EEEEWWWWWWWWWWW!!!

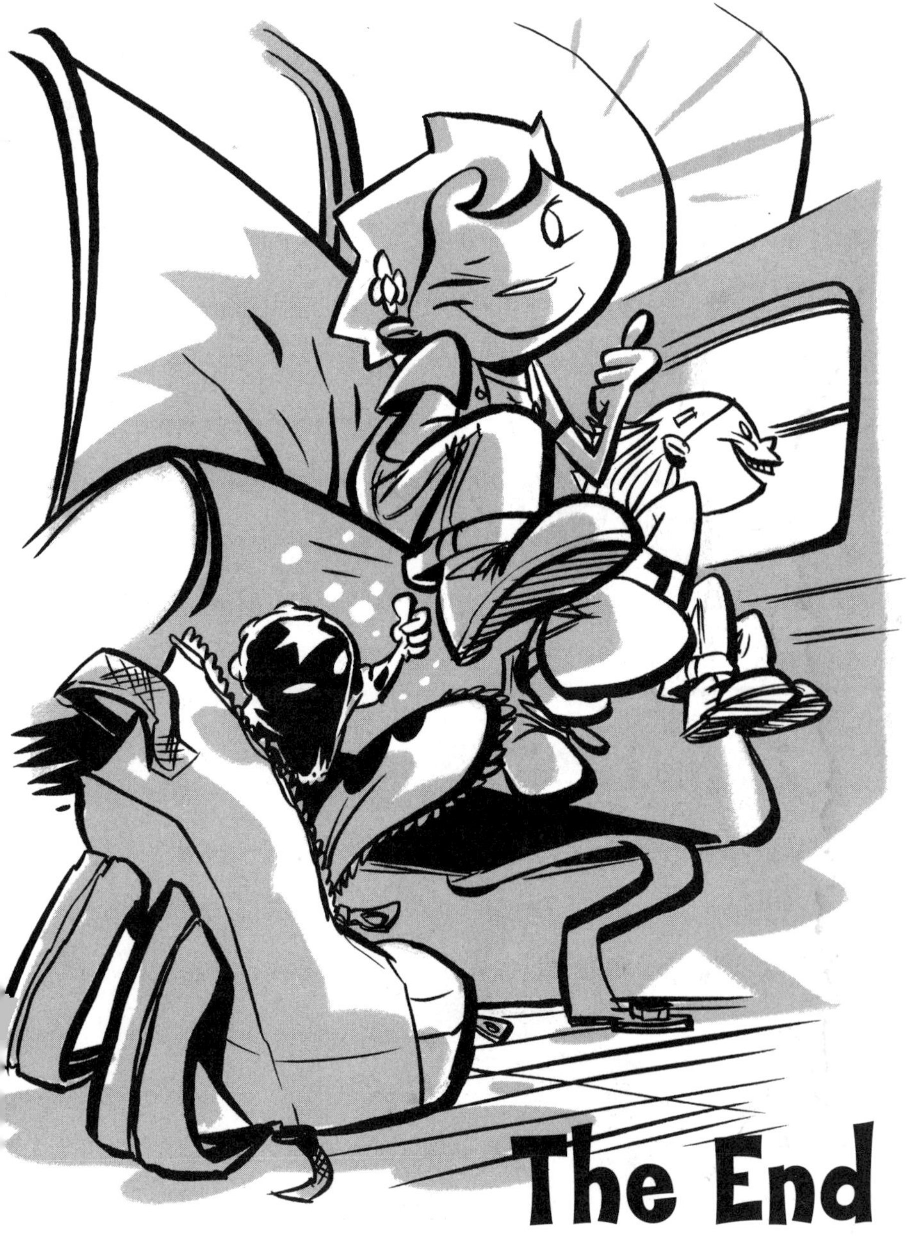
The End

MORE PICKLE POWER FROM SCHOLASTIC

Magic Pickle and Jo Jo take on the Razin', a renegade raisin with a dastardly plan: turn everybody on earth into plump, juicy, mindless grapes, so he can rule the world.

A graphix Chapter Book

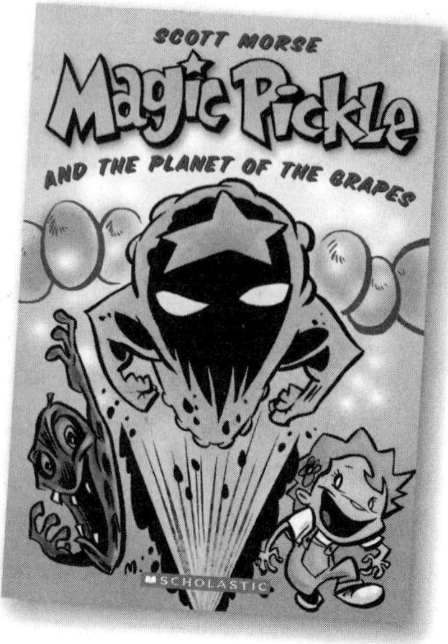
SCOTT MORSE
Magic Pickle
AND THE PLANET OF THE GRAPES
SCHOLASTIC

graphix

Available
May 2008

Here it is: the original **graphic novel** in full color!
Read the whole story behind the world's greenest,
bumpiest, briniest superhero, the Magic Pickle,
and his feisty sidekick, Jo Jo Wigman!

A thrilling, action-packed story
that starts in a secret lab and ends
in a food fight!

graphix

An Imprint of

Meet
Scott Morse

If you read Scholastic's *Goosebumps Graphix: Creepy Creatures*, you saw Scott's super-cool art in *The Abominable Snowman of Pasadena* story (and if you haven't read it, check it out!).

Scott is the award-winning author of more than ten graphic novels for children and adults, including *Soulwind*; *The Barefoot Serpent*; and *Southpaw*. He's also worked in animation for Universal, Hanna Barbera, Cartoon Network, Disney, Nickelodeon, and Pixar. Scott lives with his loving family in Northern California.

And sometimes – if there are any in the fridge – he even eats pickles.